THESE BOOTS ARE
MADE FOR STALKING

CLIQUE novels by Lisi Harrison:

THE CLIQUE

BEST FRIENDS FOR NEVER

REVENGE OF THE WANNABES

INVASION OF THE BOY SNATCHERS

THE PRETTY COMMITTEE STRIKES BACK

DIAL L FOR LOSER

IT'S NOT EASY BEING MEAN

SEALED WITH A DISS

BRATFEST AT TIFFANY'S

THE CLIQUE SUMMER COLLECTION

P.S. I LOATHE YOU

BOYS R US

CHARMED AND DANGEROUS: THE RISE OF
THE PRETTY COMMITTEE

THE CLIQUETIONARY

THESE BOOTS ARE MADE FOR STALKING

Also by Lisi Harrison:

ALPHAS

If you like THE CLIQUE, you may also enjoy:

The **Poseur** series by Rachel Maude
The **Secrets of My Hollywood Life** series by Jen Calonita

THESE BOOTS ARE
MADE FOR STALKING

A CLIQUE NOVEL BY
LISI HARRISON

poppy

LITTLE, BROWN AND COMPANY
New York   Boston

Copyright © 2010 by Alloy Entertainment

All rights reserved. Except as permitted under the U.S. Copyright Act
of 1976, no part of this publication may be reproduced, distributed, or
transmitted in any form or by any means, or stored in a database or
retrieval system, without the prior written permission of the publisher.

"Prologue/Little Shop of Horrors" by Howard Elliot Ashman, Alan Irwin Menken (Universal
Geffen Music, Menken Music, Trunksong Music LTD). All rights reserved.

"Suddenly Seymour" by Howard Elliot Ashman, Alan Irwin Menken (Universal Geffen Music,
Menken Music, Trunksong Music LTD). All rights reserved.

Poppy

Little, Brown and Company
Hachette Book Group
237 Park Avenue, New York, NY 10017
For more of your favorite series, go to www.pickapoppy.com

First Edition: March 2010

Poppy is an imprint of Little, Brown and Company.
The Poppy name and logo are trademarks of Hachette Book Group, Inc.

The characters and events in this book are fictitious. Any similarity to real
persons, living or dead, is coincidental and not intended by the author.

CLIQUE® is a registered trademark of Alloy Media, LLC.

Cover design by Andrea C. Uva
Cover photos by Roger Moenks
Author photo by Gillian Crane

alloy**entertainment**
Produced by Alloy Entertainment
151 West 26th Street, New York, NY 10001

ISBN: 978-0-316-00683-5

10 9 8 7 6 5 4 3 2 1
CWO
Printed in the United States of America

For Bee Bee, the ah-dorable four-legged inspiration for Bark Obama and Bean Block.

And, of course, Meg Haston. You are truly ah-mazing.

"Rate my costume," Massie Block demanded, spinning around in a circle so the Pretty Committee could see her black silk Theory jumpsuit and red patent-leather Brian Atwood pumps from every angle. Hands on hips, she ran her tongue over her fang-enhanced smile and dared her friends to give her anything less than a 9.2.

Alicia Rivera and Dylan Marvil conferred like they were front-row fashion critics and Merri-Lee Marvil's two-story walk-in closet was the main tent at Bryant Park. Dylan's mom had given the girls permission to accessorize their Halloween costumes with anything from her closet that had passed the BEST IF WORN BY tags dangling from their hangers.

Claire Lyons flashed a pointy-eye-toothed grin. "Nine-point-eight!"

"Heart it." Alicia applauded.

"To *die* for." Kristen Gregory grabbed a lacy camisole that hung from the crystal wall sconce like a cobweb.

"Suuuuuuuck iiiiit, Bellllaaaaahhhh," Dylan burped, reaching for another chewy ghost PEEP.

Without warning, an electric shiver shimmied down Massie's spine. Maybe it was the sting of her new lip-plumping Glossip Girl Bite Me Berry stain. Maybe it was the eerie flicker of the Belle Fleur Cacao Tabaq soy candles Dylan had lit to get her friends in the Halloween spirit. Or maybe it was the thrill of knowing that the Pretty Committee was back together and tighter than Massie's abs after a two-hour Zumba-thon.

Alicia lifted her palm and Massie leaned down to victory-five it. When their palms met, waves of understanding flowed between them. Without saying a word, it was clear that Alicia would never try to be the alpha of her own clique again, like she'd done with the Soul-M8s, her failed boy-girl clique. And Massie would try to be a little less Bumble & Bumble super-hold hairspray and a little more Frederic Fekkai flexible hold.

"Are you sure Landon won't think it's juvenile?" Massie asked, adjusting her black lace gloves. Now that she had an ah-dorable, fashion-savvy ninth-grade crush, the margin for fashion error was slimmer than a pair of J Brand Skinny jeans.

"Did you ask him to go trick-or-treating yet?" Kristen pushed herself to her feet, then teetered to the far wall in platform Jimmy Choos to riffle through the hanging clothes. Polaroids of Merri-Lee wearing the outfits hung from the hangers, expiration dates inked in red.

"Not officially," Massie admitted. "But we've been texting about hanging out tomorrow night. He's probably just waiting for me to let him know the plan." She nibbled her bottom lip, wishing she could sneak a quick text check.

"Josh's been tweeting all week about how pumped he is to

see me in my costume." Alicia reached for a blood orange slice and popped it in her mouth.

"Derrington's definitely coming," Dylan announced, pretending to examine her flat-ironed red locks for split ends.

"Good." Massie flashed a reassuring smile, to prove she was fine with Dylan and Kristen crushing on her exes. So getting two of her crushes stolen had left her with more trust issues than the U.S. Treasury. But thanks to her new subliminal confidence-building CD, *Surviving Male Betrayal,* she was guaranteed to lose those issues faster than Nicole Richie shed her baby weight. Or else Oprah and her book club would have some serious explaining to do.

Just then, a deep, evil laugh boomed from the intercom. "MUUUUUUUUAAAAAHHHHHHAAAAAAAAAAAAAHH-HAAAAAAAAA."

"Ahhhhhhhhhhhhhhhhhhhhhhhhhhhhhhhhhhh!" the whole PC screamed. Claire panic-flung a gummy foot across the room. Dylan grabbed the top off a Prada shoe box and held it in front of her like a shield. And Bean, Massie's black pug, leapt off a bed of Hermès silk scarves and made a beeline for Massie, her red silk cape fluttering behind her like she was an ah-dorable superhero.

"Bean!" Massie swooped down to rescue her puppy. Bean's custom white fangs tipped with OPI's Vampire State Building polish chattered in fear.

Seconds later, Layne Abeley appeared in the arched double doorway in a GHOULS JUST WANNA HAVE FUN T-shirt and neon orange skinny jeans.

"Ehmagawd, Layne!" Massie said, her heart racing in her chest. "You almost gave Bean a heart attack!"

"Sorrrrrry." Layne plopped down next to Claire like she belonged there.

The PC insta-grabbed their phones.

Dylan: K, did u invite Layne?
Kristen: Nope. U?
Alicia: The shirt sucks.
Dylan: And the pants bite. ☺
Massie: Outfit should b 6 ft under. ☺
Dylan: Wonder if C invited her?
Massie: Probs. Just ignore her.

Massie took a giant gulp of her Draculatte to wash down the guilt lump starting to form in her throat. The truth was that when Layne had complained in second-period French about not having a costume, Massie had mentioned where the PC would be after school. Which meant she'd semi-invited the LBR. But she hadn't *really* had a choice. When Dylan and Kristen had stolen ex-Derrington and ex-Dempsey, Layne had produced her brother Chris Abeley's ninth-grade friends. Including Landon Crane.

But most important, when Massie had been forced to hire actors for her new clique to make the old one jealous, Layne hadn't told a soul (or a Soul-M8).

"What're you guys supposed to be anyway?" Layne piped up, double-knotting the green glitter laces on her black Converse sneakers.

Dylan rolled her eyes. "We're going as trampires."

"Huh?" Layne's under-plucked brows inched toward each other as she helped herself to the tray of bite-size brownies, blood oranges, and dark chocolate–covered popcorn.

"Trampires," Alicia repeated, tightening the silver braided belt she wore over a strapless slate gray Alexander Wang dress. "Hawt vampires." She'd ripped holes in a pair of Merri-Lee's DKNY fishnets and painted tiny bite marks on her leg with a scarlet YSL lip liner. "Genius, right? Massie thought of it."

Dylan smile-thanked Massie for the idea before yanking down the hem of her black Cosabella slip.

Massie beamed *You're welcome.* This year, every girl in eighth was either dressing up like Bella Swan or one of the Cullen girls, which meant the vampire trend was deader than dead. So she'd added an alpha twist.

"I get the tramp part." Layne inspected Claire's lace-trimmed burgundy slip. "But what's the 'pire' part?"

"We're not spray-tanning this year," Massie explained. "So we'll be super-pale."

"Come on, Layne," Claire said. "Let's go find you a costume." She pushed herself to her feet, then gripped Layne's hands and pulled her up too.

"Okay. But nothing trampy." She followed Claire up the spiral staircase to the second floor.

"Style-sucker," Alicia called after them. Her dark hair looked glossier than usual in the candlelight.

"Ah-greed," Massie giggled, settling on the floor next to

Kristen. Being back together with her friends felt better than one of Jakkob's post-highlight scalp massages. She pinky-swore to herself that she would never let crush issues crush the Pretty Committee again.

Massie's iPhone buzzed again.

Landon: Is Bean up 4 a date w/Bark 2morrow nite?

"Ehmacrush!" Massie giggle-beamed at her iPhone. She pulled Bean into her lap, fingering the silver charms that hung from the pug's purple silk charm collar. The collar had been a gift from Landon and his pug, Bark Obama. Bean refused to go anywhere without it.

Kristen and Alicia dove toward Massie's cell.

"Whasshesay?" Dylan wobbled across the closet and crouched behind Massie.

"You're so gonna lip-kiss tomorrow night," Alicia predicted.

"Prah-bly," Massie said coyly, even though the thought of lip-kissing an older man made her gloss sweat.

Bean jumped from Massie's lap and scampered in hyper circles around the girls, her tiny pink tongue flapping in the cacao-scented air.

"Hey!" Layne bellowed, bending over the railing above. She was wearing a long red silk bathrobe. "I'm Little Dead Riding Hood!" Claire was drawing bloody gashes on Layne's face with a cheap Wet N Wild lip liner.

Massie held up a hand, silencing the chatter, then fired back a reply.

Massie: Paws-ibly. ☺ Bring Bark by my house at 7:45. Trick-or-treating starts at 8.
Landon: Can't. Movie scare-a-thon @ a friend's. Wanna join?

"He wants me to hang out with his friends," Massie said slowly. Her Draculatte swirled violently in her stomach.

Dylan's dark chocolate–stained lips melted into a thin, pursed line. "What're you gonna do?"

Bean stopped mid-circle and rapid-blinked at Massie.

Alicia and Kristen leaned forward slightly, begging her with wide eyes not to ditch them for her crush. Bean pleaded to see Bark, her black eyes round and moist with hope. *"Bark!"* she yapped, in case Massie didn't get the point.

Massie reached for her latte, stalling for time. On the one hand, the thought of Landon not seeing her in her trampire costume made her blood run cold. On the other hand, hadn't she just pinky-sworn to herself that she would never let a crush crush the Pretty Committee?

The drops of red food coloring staining the frothy white latte foam in her cup caught Massie's eye, reminding her that she and the PC weren't just friends. They were like blood-sisters. And blood-sisters didn't desert their friends for boys. Not even if those boys were fashion-loving, pug-owning, ninth-grade-attending hawties.

She swallowed. "I'm obviously going trick-or-treating," she said definitively, as if she'd never considered another option.

Dylan, Kristen, and Alicia breathed a sigh of relief, then fanned out to complete their costumes. Bean sulk-yapped, collapsing on the floor in defeat.

Before Massie could change her mind, she texted Landon.

Massie: Can't. Trick-or-treating w/the girls. Bean = ☹.

Massie felt like someone was stiletto-stabbing her in the heart, then filling the hole with a million insecurities. She re-glossed quickly, to seal them in.

Bean lifted her head hopefully at the sound of Massie's buzzing phone.

Landon: Wanna bring Bean 2 the scare-a-thon?
At least the puppies can hang. I'll chaperone.

Massie paused. She'd never let Bean out of her sight for an entire night before. But then again . . .

"Bean!" she said. "Want me to drop you off at Bark's tomorrow?"

Bean leapt up and barreled full-force into Massie's lap, her charm collar jangling happily.

Massie giggled, breathing in the warm scent of her puppy's customized vanilla bean shampoo. At least if Massie couldn't be with her crush on Halloween, Bean could be with hers. And if dropping Bean off at Landon's led to a) Landon witnessing Massie looking ah-mazing in her trampire costume, b) Landon ditching his friends in favor of trick-or-treating with the PC, or c) Landon vowing never to leave Massie's side again, then so be it.

Besides, there were other perks. Massie scratched underneath Bean's collar, pinching the tiny silver dog-bone charm between her index finger and thumb. The charm was a Snoop-Dawg; it had a tiny camera inside that sent a video feed to the SnoopDawg Web site so pet owners could monitor their pets 24/7. All Massie had to do was activate the charm and check the site from her iPhone tomorrow night, and she could watch Bean's every move.

And Landon's.

Massie giggle-grinned to herself, feeling her insecurities retreat. It was the perfect way to keep an eye on her new crush. She knew it was sneaky, but who cared? She'd promised to work on her trust issues. And she would.

Starting Monday.

CURRENT STATE OF THE UNION	
IN	**OUT**
Trampires	Vampires
Friday, Oct. 31st	Friday the 13th
SnoopDawg charm collar	Tiffany & Co. charm bracelet

Claire Lyons linked arms with Massie, who linked arms with Alicia, who linked arms with Kristen, who linked arms with Dylan. Together, Claire and her fellow trampires charged through the darkness toward the first house of the night, Guerlain-powdered faces deathly pale and Crest Whitestripped fangs gleaming. David and Victoria Beckham, a Masai bushman, a bloody-fanged ump-pire, and Chewbacca from *Star Wars* followed close behind. The *click-clack* of the girls' heels on the pavement pierced the crisp night air, sending clusters of drugstore costume–wearing amateurs scrambling out of the way.

"Caaaaaaaannnndy," Dylan droned like a zombie, staring down the driveway that led to a looming Tudor-style mansion. Smoke from the glowing paper luminaries lining the drive mixed with the warm smells of melted caramel, burnt marsh-mallows, and Massie's signature Chanel No. 19 perfume.

Goosebumps prickled Claire's bare arms, but she was too excited to care. Her gray fleece didn't exactly go with Merri-Lee Marvil's burgundy D&G slip dress and black satin Ferrag-amo peep-toes. And claiming the chills would give Claire the perfect excuse later to snuggle up to her crush, Cam Fisher.

"Guh-ross." Alicia flashed her fangs as the PC led their

crushes and Layne around a tiered stone fountain in front of the estate. Hundreds of rubber eyeballs bobbed in the churning water, which had been dyed dark red to look like blood.

"*Huuarughhhh,*" grunted Layne from beneath her rubber Chewbacca mask. Her brown, feather-covered unitard was stuffed with fluffy down pillows for extra padding.

Claire giggled, secretly loving that Layne had turned down her offer to be a trampire so she could dress like Chewie.

"Sweet!" Derrington yelled, rushing the fountain and scooping a handful of the painted rubber eyeballs from the water. "Ammo!"

Dylan rolled her eyes, but a smile twitched at the corners of her mouth as Derrington punted the spheres at Dempsey.

"Hey!" Dempsey swung at the eyeballs with the ten-foot spear he'd used to accessorize his tiny red loincloth. "My mom got this at a tribal ceremony in Africa! She'll kill you if it gets messed up."

"And she'll kill *you* if she realizes her skirt's missing from her display case," Kristen chided her crush, tugging at the pewter Undrest chemise she wore over lumpy metallic leggings; she had a ski suit on under her costume in case she ran into her mom and had to do a quick change. The overall effect was more sumo wrestler than sexy trampire.

Out of eyeballs, Derrington ran back over and punched Josh-slash-Victoria Beckham in the shoulder. "Dude, this is a family show. Keep it clean."

"Huh?" Josh Spice glanced down. Without Alicia's C-cups to hold it in place, the black strapless minidress he'd borrowed from her was starting to inch down his chest. "Whoops. I guess I need a smaller size." He grinned, cracking the perma-Posh-frown he'd painted on with lip liner.

Alicia's cheeks flushed to match her Stila-stained pout. "It'sbigonmetoo."

Cam let out a quiet snicker and Claire elbowed him swiftly in the ribs. Not that she was actually mad. Even in an umpire mask and blood-tipped fangs, Cam looked adorable. The furry bat on his shoulder had been Claire's idea, and it was the perfect finishing touch for his ump-pire costume.

"Claire, are you a judge on *Dancing with the Stars*?" Massie's voice jolted Claire from her Cam-coma. Or, as Massie liked to call it, her Cam-a.

"Nope."

"Then quit checking Cam's every move." Massie resumed her strut, leading the girls and their crushes toward the house.

Busted. Claire grinned, relieved that Massie was in a good mood despite being crush-minus for the night. She was even more relieved that the Pretty Committee was finally back to normal. And it was partly thanks to her. When she'd figured out that Massie had hired actors for her new crew, Claire had taken matters into her own hands. She'd secretly convinced the actors to act clingier than a cheap jersey dress so Massie would realize who her true friends were. And now the PC was back and stronger than Zac and Vanessa.

When they reached the end of the driveway, Dylan whipped her red feather boa around her neck with a flourish and tromped up the stone steps toward the arched wooden door.

Claire burst out laughing at the sight of a very tiny Luke Skywalker coming down the steps, swishing a neon light saber at an imaginary opponent.

"*Huuuuuuuuuargh,*" Chewie squealed.

"Layne," Massie snapped, the tips of her fangs showing slightly. "English, puh-lease."

Chewie swung her wrinkly rubber face in Claire's direction.

"Method acting," Claire explained. "She can't break character."

Massie rolled her kohl-lined eyes. "Actors," she said, just loud enough for Dempsey to hear. Then she planted her Chanel Black Satin–polished nail on the doorbell, and a ghoulish wail echoed inside the dark entryway.

Seconds later, a silver-haired man in a cornflower blue cardigan and a neon green Frankenstein mask answered the door. A giant glass bowl overflowing with colorfully wrapped goodies was cradled under his left arm.

"Trick-or-treeeeeeaaaat," Claire bellowed along with her friends.

Except for Massie, who was sneaking a peek at her iPhone.

And Chewie, who grunted, "*Huuua huuaaaarrghhhhh!*"

The trampires extended their bags. They'd chosen the roomiest designer totes they owned, to maximize candy-filling potential. The boys and Layne had brought Hefty garbage bags.

"Well," a muffled, grandfatherly voice leaked from the

rubber mask. "Aren't you all"—the mask surveyed the trampires' barely there costumes—"something."

"Given." Alicia beamed.

"Fill 'er up," Dylan interrupted, elbowing her way to the front door and yanking open the black patent Versace rolling trolley she used for overnight trips.

Frankenstein peered skeptically inside the suitcase, then dropped a tin of chocolate hazelnut espresso beans into the empty tote. It landed with a hollow thud.

"Thanks." Dylan didn't budge.

Frankenstein took the hint, digging a small gold box of chocolates and a pack of colorful gummies from the bowl. He dropped those in the bag too. Claire's mouth watered and she shifted impatiently in her peep-toes.

"Dylan." Massie had stashed her iPhone back in her bag. "Are you a Barney's twenty-four-hour sale?"

Dylan shook her head, sending her professionally straightened locks swinging in a shimmering velvet curtain around her shoulders.

Massie glanced at Alicia, Claire, and Kristen.

"'Cause you're taking ALL DAY!" the girls cackled, hip-bumping Dylan out of the way.

Claire tried not to gawk as Frankenstein filled the rest of the PC's designer candy bags. Comparing Halloween in Orlando to Halloween in Westchester was like comparing Keds to Kors. Here, Claire's tote was filled with chocolates from the Godiva G collection, Dean & Deluca butter caramels, and gummy vampire fangs from Dylan's Candy Bar. In Florida, the best Claire could hope for in her plastic pumpkin was a mini Snickers. Once, she'd gotten a tube of denture cream.

Yip! Yip! Yip!

Massie blushed under her pressed powder and hugged her bag to her chest.

"What was that?" Claire demanded as they made their way down the steps.

"What was what?" Massie asked lightly. They passed a gaggle of sixth-graders dressed as the cast of *High School Musical* who were pelting one another with reject candy. Ducking to avoid taking a cellophane-wrapped candy apple to the head, Claire furrowed her brow at Massie's tote.

"Your bag barked." Claire cocked her head slightly to the right, staring directly into Massie's eyes. It was the same look Massie gave Alicia when she suspected her of withholding good gossip.

"Puh-lease. I invented that look." Massie shook her head, staring over Claire's shoulder into the chilly darkness.

But Claire had learned from the best and she refused to look away.

Massie sighed. "Fine," she said, unzipping her bag and pulling out her iPhone. "It's the SnoopDawg Web site. It barks every time Bean shifts positions." She tilted the phone in Claire's direction.

"Uh . . . I don't see anything," Claire said into the black screen.

"I know," Massie huffed. "The charm got twisted around or something. It's recording Bean's throat."

Claire shook her head, swallowing a giggle. "Come on," she coaxed. "Put the phone away. Bean's fine."

"Fine." Massie chucked her phone into her bag. "Happy?" But the gleam in her amber eyes proved she wasn't really mad.

"Let's move, people," Dylan interrupted. "There's still six houses on this street."

Claire and Massie linked arms with Alicia, Dylan, and Kristen and turned to go.

"Wait. Where'd the boys go?" Alicia sucked in her breath and stopped dead in her tracks, yanking Claire and the rest of girls to a halt. Keeping her elbow locked with Claire's, she dragged the PC chain in a 180-degree turn, making them look like the Rockettes prepping for their finale in the middle of the driveway.

Claire squint-searched for Cam. "Um, there." She pointed to the front lawn, where her crush, the rest of the boys, and Layne were rearranging a giant spider lawn ornament in the yard to make it look like it was humping a defenseless jack-o'-lantern. Claire blushed.

Kristen sighed.

Alicia lowered her eyes to the pavement.

"Come on. The boys'll catch up later," Massie ordered, steering them toward the street.

At least it's dark, Claire thought to herself, embarrassed for their crushes and Layne. Maybe no one would recognize Cam in his ump-pire mask. Josh Spice, on the other hand . . .

"Hotz! Hotz! Hotz!" Suddenly the boys sprinted past the

PC, egging Josh on as he ran barefoot into the street. He held the giant lawn spider over his head like an Olympic trophy.

"My pumps!" Alicia wailed, speed-leading the PC in the boys' wake. "Those were vintage!"

Behind them, Layne pity-patted Alicia's shoulder with a hairy paw.

"*Yip! Yip! Yip!*" Bean's bark leaked from Massie's bag again. She reached for her phone. Again.

Massie stare-silenced Claire before she could say a word. "It just so happens, Kuh-laire, that this is the longest Bean and I have ever been apart. What kind of mother would I be if I didn't—"

"No lights." Josh huffed as the girls caught up to them in front of the next house on the street. He bent over like he was cramping from too many soccer sprints.

"And no decorations," Dempsey shuddered, his bare legs starting to turn a grayish-purple in the cold.

"Which means no good candy." Dylan leaned against her rolling suitcase, narrowing her eyes at the modest two-story brick house in front of them. A single, unlit jack-o'-lantern sagged on the front stoop.

"Steeeeeeeer-ike three!" Cam called, baring his fangs.

Claire's heart fluttered in her chest.

"Opposite of worth it," Alicia decided after a quick re-gloss.

"Skip it," Kristen declared.

"No way," Claire said firmly. "N.H.L.B."

"N.H.L.B.?" Kristen echoed.

"No House Left Behind," Claire explained. "That means we hit every house, every year. No exceptions."

Cam's blue eye filled with admiration. So did his green one.

"We're not in it for the candy, Kuh-laire," Massie said dismissively. "We're in it for the costumes." She crossed her arms over her jumpsuit.

"I'minitforboth," Dylan clarified.

Claire shrugged at Massie. "Whatevs," she said, Cam's encouragement fueling her like a mid-morning gummy fix. She stepped onto the front lawn, her satin-covered heels immediately sinking into the grass.

Dylan popped another fistful of espresso beans, then leapt onto the lawn. "Coming!"

Layne grunted her approval, lumbering slowly behind Dylan. Cam and the boys followed.

"This better be good," Massie sighed.

Claire led her friends though the cold, wet grass, exhilarated. Last year, Massie definitely wouldn't have given in to her so easily. It felt like catching Massie without gloss in the morning—a rare moment of vulnerability. Or maybe the alpha was finally letting go of her Lycra ways.

Claire was the first to reach the door. An orange plastic bowl filled with candy sat on the front steps of the dark house, and a handwritten sign was taped to the bowl.

TAKE WHATEVER YOU WANT. THEN LEAVE.

"Done and done." Just as Claire was about to dig into the bowl, flickering lights to her left caught her eye. In a glass-enclosed sunroom off the side of the house, a giant flat screen broadcast a larger-than-life image of Janet Leigh showering in the Bates Motel.

"Move it or lose it, Kuh-laire." Massie and the other trampires crowded onto the stoop.

"It's *Psycho*!" Claire said, pointing to the TV. "My all-time favorite horror—"

"Ahhhhhhhhhhhhhhhhhhhhh!" High-pitched screams erupted from inside, and bright white light from the screen illuminated a group of girls and guys crammed onto a leather sofa together. Two tiny puppies were curled up in a bowl on one of the girls' laps.

Claire froze at the sight of three very familiar faces:

Landon Crane. Bean Block. And Bark Obama.

On the screen, a dark, knife-wielding figure appeared behind the white curtain. Blood swirled down the drain. But the horror on-screen was nothing compared to the scene unfolding next to Claire.

Massie's eyes narrowed and her fangs gleamed in the blue light. Claire's heart plunged lower than Josh's neckline. Landon Crane had no idea, but his Halloween scare-a-thon was about to get seriously terrifying.

Massie trudged through the holly bushes separating the front door from the sunroom. The spiky leaves felt like a million knives stabbing her calves with every step. But compared to the pain in her heart, the prickly leaves might as well have been tiny puppy tongues lapping at her wounds.

"Eh," Alicia breathed behind her.

"Ma," Kristen huffed.

"Gaaaawwwrrrrr," Dylan managed over a mouthful of dark chocolate caramels.

Massie felt her already deathly pale cheeks turning Q-tip white. She wanted to scream, to curl up underneath her duvet and inhale every piece of Halloween candy she could find without even bothering to calorie count. Instead, she just stared through the window, watching the scene in front of her play out like a low-budget horror flick on mute.

Inside, Landon was sandwiched on the sofa between two blond girls who were more tanned than Massie's leather Hype Agyness tote. Miles and Ace, Landon's buddies who'd modeled at Massie's Ho Ho Homeless benefit, were wedged on either side of the girls. And Scott, a.k.a. DJ Re-Quest, who'd saved the day by DJ'ing the benefit, was stretched out on the floor. Bean and Bark were snuggling in a giant bowl of candy corn.

Massie's throat cinched tight. She tried to swallow the betrayal rising like a lump from her stomach, but it was impossible. How could Landon cuddle with two girls who weren't Massie on the most romantic night of the year? And in front of Bean!

An ice-cold hand gripped Massie's shoulder.

"What?" she whisper-snapped. Bronze and Bronzer were snuggling even closer to Landon, the hems on their too-short minis inching up their thighs. What were they dressed up as? Desperate?

"You okay?" Claire's voice sounded muted over the sound of Massie's heart drumming in her ears. "This is totally my fault."

"Gawd, Claire, not everything is about you," Massie hissed without tearing her gaze from the window. Even though she did blame Claire, a little. But mostly she blamed herself for handing her heart to Landon so he could shred it like a pair of Rich and Skinny distressed boyfriend jeans.

Just then, the brassy blonde to Landon's right squealed at the screen, flirt-burying her orange face in Landon's shoulder. "Maybe those girls are, like, Landon's sisters," Kristen whispered hopefully. The trail mix on her breath smelled like pity.

As if sensing Massie's despair, Bean sat up suddenly. Her nose sniffed the air and her eyes zeroed in on the window. She leapt out of the candy bowl, hurtling toward Massie. A second later, she careened into the glass-paned door with a thud.

"Beeeeaaaan!" Massie wailed, pressing her fingers against

the tiny snot smudge on the window. Bean staggered backward, shaking her head from side to side. The PC dropped to the ground behind Massie and dragged Layne down with them. On the lawn, the boys snickered.

Startled, Landon looked up from the movie and squinted directly at Massie. Rushing over to the window, he picked up Bean and cradled her in his arms, Bark speed-circling his caramel Puma Black Labels.

Massie? Landon mouthed silently from the other side of the glass.

As casually as possible, Massie leaned against the window and flicked her flat-ironed locks over one shoulder, as if to say, *Oh, heyyyyy. I was totally just in the neighborhood. Weird running into each other like this, right? Love the sneakers, by the way. Oh, and if you let those girls touch my puppy, I'll show you a real-life* Psycho.

Landon motioned for Massie to go around to the front door. Then his eyes slid down to the ground, where Dylan, Alicia, Kristen, and Layne were still crouched at Massie's feet.

"Thinkheseesus?" Dylan muttered.

"Thedoorisglass," Claire murmured back.

"Ehmagawd, would you guys get up?" Massie snapped, stomping through the prickly bushes. The holly leaves dug into her jumpsuit, as if trying to hold her back. She ignored them, hurrying along the edge of the lawn to the front door. The rest of the PC, Layne, and the boys fell in behind her.

When she reached the front of the house, Landon was standing underneath a flickering porch light in the doorway, still cradling Bean. The puppy practically flew from Landon's arms into Massie's the second she saw her.

"Hua hua huarrgh," Layne shrieked, glaring down at Bark Obama, who was humping her feather-covered leg.

"He's a major *Star Wars* fan," Landon laughed, the skin around his bluish-green eyes crinkling in the most irresistible way. When he focused them on Massie, she dropped Bean to the brick steps and leaned against the doorframe. It was partly to look sexy but mainly to keep herself upright.

Massie snuck a peek at Landon's eyes. Even in the dark, they seemed to change color every few seconds. Now they looked exactly the same color as the ocean water in St. Barts. Instantly, the anger she'd felt toward Landon for ditching her on Halloween evaporated like cheap lip gloss.

"Wanna come in? We're just watching a movie." Landon looked quizzically over Massie's shoulder at her entourage, lifting his hand in a wave.

"Sure!" Massie grinned. Immediately, she cursed herself for not acting like she might have had something better to do. Behind her, the Pretty Committee exchanged glances. Why was it that one look at Landon made her forget how to act alpha?

"Awesome." Landon led the group through the dark foyer and into the sunroom, where the girls, Miles, Ace, and Scott were still glued to the movie. The tiny room smelled like cheap vanilla body spray, sugar, and warm puppy. Massie's eyes slid from the worn sisal rug to the pilled Aztec-patterned throw draped over the back of the worn leather sofa. A decorative clay urn held the door open. Had Landon seriously turned down a night of trick-or-treating with the PC to hang in a room decorated in early American tacky?

"You guys remember Massie. And her friends," Landon announced.

Scott lifted his hand from the candy corn bowl to wave. "What up." He dropped his hand back in the bowl.

Miles and Ace nodded.

"And that's Brianna and Liz," Landon said, wrapping up introductions.

The girls glanced up briefly, then returned to the movie, ignoring Massie completely. On the flat screen, Norman Bates looked ready to go on a killing spree. Massie could sympathize.

"Hey." Massie nodded at no one in particular. Her head was starting to throb from the overwhelming combination of cheap body spray and self-righteous ninth-grade beta.

The rest of the trampires half-waved, bouncing awkwardly in their heels like they had to pee.

"Trick-or-treaters," Brianna muttered under her breath. "How cute. Candy's by the door."

The boys glanced at Landon, Miles, Ace, and Scott, who were all in street clothes, and reddened. Derrington was staring at the cashmere throw on the couch like he'd trade his Xbox and his Pro Evolution Soccer 2009 game just to have something to cover his bare chest.

"Remember when we used to go trick-or-treating?" Liz murmured, dragging the throw over the back of the couch and wrapping herself in it.

"Not really," Brianna shrugged. "It was kind of a long time ago." She side-glanced at Massie. "Vampires. How original."

Massie's stomach twisted into a giant Twizzler. Next to these girls, she looked paler than Kristen Stewart in January. Did Landon like girls who were super-tan? Was it too late to sneak a quick cheek-pinch?

Massie swallowed her insecurities, leveling her gaze at Brianna's carrot-colored face. "Are you dressed as a statue?"

Brianna rolled her eyes. "No," she said, a flicker of uncertainty passing over her face.

"Then why are you so bronzed?" Massie fired back.

Landon busted out laughing. Even Scott, Ace, and Miles cracked a smile.

And Bean and Bark ran victory laps around Massie's feet.

The Pretty Committee, Layne, and Landon raised their palms for a round of high fives. Massie could feel a confidence comeback on the way. As she sashayed down the line, high-fiving her friends, she wondered whether she should slap Landon's palm hard, like she meant it, or soft, in a more feminine—

Suddenly, her left heel caught in a loop in the sisal carpet, and she dove forward, her hands clawing desperately at the vanilla-scented air. It was as if someone had TiVo'd her public humiliation, and was playing it back in excruciating slo-mo. She caught a glimpse of Dylan's widened emerald eyes and glossy lips, which were parting in horror as the gap between Massie and the carpet narrowed.

"Nooooooooooooooooooooooooooooooooooooooooooooooo!" Dylan's voice sounded far away, like she was yelling underwater.

Her stomach bottoming out, Massie threw her right leg forward to break her fall.

A long, pained squeal rose up from the floor, and Massie looked down in time to see her heel piercing Bark Obama's paw.

"Yiiiiiiiiiiiiiiiiiiiiiiiiiipppppppppp!"

"Ehhhhhhhhhhhhhhhhhhhhhhhhhhhhhhhhhhhhhmagaaaaaaa-aaaaaaaaaaaaaaaaaaaaaaaaawd," Massie screamed.

Kristen's nails grip-dug into Massie's arms, pulling her off the pug.

"Bark!" Panic pulsed in Landon's eyes as he swooped down to rescue his puppy.

"Bark! I'm so sorry!" Massie shook free of Kristen's grasp and dropped to her knees, reaching for Bark's shaking paw.

"No!" Landon pulled Bark away, shielding him from Massie like he was a precious designer tote and she was Winona Ryder on a shoplifting spree.

Massie hurt-widened her amber eyes.

"I mean . . . it's fine," Landon said quickly. "He'll be fine. It was an accident." But his eyes were stormy, like the Caribbean during hurricane season.

Massie tried to meet his gaze, but he was too busy soothe-petting Bark to notice. Her heart, and her confidence, sank through the floor.

A tiny smile twitched at the corners of Brianna's mouth

as she watched Landon tending to Bark. Shifting her attention to Massie, she narrowed her eyes. "Um, isn't it past your bedtime?"

Massie wanted to strangle her with Bean's collar. But instead, she whirled around on her heel, signaling to her friends that it was time to go.

"I'll check on Bark tomorrow," she whispered, too ashamed to look at Landon. She picked up Bean and tucked the pug under her damp, stress-stained armpit.

"Nighty-night," Brianna said dryly.

"Text you later," Landon said halfheartedly, without looking up.

The PC and their crushes were silent as Massie stalked out of the house and through the yard. Tears threatened to spill onto her pale cheeks, but she refused to let two orange-tinted LBRs make her cry. She hugged Bean to her chest and tried to put on a brave face.

But how was she supposed to do that when her puppy smelled like some ninth-grader's cheap perfume?

"Oof." The thick strap of Claire's borrowed Jimmy Choo Sky bag dug into her shoulder as she lugged her loot across Massie's white-carpeted bedroom floor toward the sleeping bag circle in the middle of the room. Every muscle in her neck, arms, and shoulders throbbed from the weight of the night's stash. But Claire felt about trick-or-treating the same way Massie felt about her *Ab Blaster* workout DVD: If you couldn't feel the burn, you weren't doing it right.

"Which is worse?" Sitting cross-legged at the head of her sleeping bag, Alicia was studying the label on a tin of pumpkin spice malt balls. "Trans fat or saturated fat?"

Dylan plopped down on her hunter green sleeping bag, then slapped a palmful of gourmet popcorn to her mouth. "Traaaaaaans faaaaaaaaat," she burped.

"Guh-ross." Kristen lifted her Juicy Couture cotton nightie over her nose. "Jalapeño?"

"*Sí.*" Dylan nodded happily.

"I'm trading anything with this many calories anyway." Alicia resumed calculating protein-to-fat ratios on her iPhone.

"How come Layne went home so early?" Kristen turned to Claire.

"Wardrobe malfunction." Claire dropped her bag to the

floor and eased into her usual spot between Kristen and Dylan. "Her costume gave her a rash, so she had to go home and take an oatmeal bath."

Dylan snorted.

Alicia wrinkled her button nose. "That's what she gets for going synthetic," she decided, pointing and flexing her feet absently.

"Poor Chewie." Kristen smile-braided a few blond layers, then finger-combed her hair and started over again.

Drawing her knees to her chest, Claire watched as Dylan snuck a mini Twix and Alicia admired her polished toes. It was moments like this that made Claire want to pinch herself, just to be sure she was actually here, in Massie Block's bedroom, hanging with the Pretty Committee like things had always been this way. Like she belonged.

She flinched at the memory of last year's costume. What had she been thinking, co-hosting a Halloween party dressed as a Powerpuff Girl? Of course, last Halloween hadn't been *all* bad. After all, she'd met her ah-dorable crush. And she was here now and she finally belonged. Now that the PC was reunited and Massie's Friday-night sleepovers were back to normal, everything was perfect. Except . . .

Claire eyed Massie's empty lilac sleeping bag and her fluffed pillow, where Bean was curled up in a ball. On the other side of the room, Massie was sitting on the edge of her bed, jamming her iPod onto the sleek portable dock on her nightstand. Her candy bag sat untouched next to her.

"We can't start withoooout you," Claire sang, trying to

sound upbeat. She tried to get a read on Massie's mood. But Massie's flat-ironed tresses were shielding her expression like a silky chestnut curtain.

"You guys go ahead," Massie murmured. "Be right there."

"You sure?" Claire nibbled her thumbnail. If it weren't for her stupid N.H.L.B. rule, the sleeping bag circle would be complete. But instead, she'd led Massie into certain heartbreak. Crushed by her crush, she'd probably slip into a deep depression for the rest of her teenage years. And it would be all Claire's fault, for dragging her friends to that darkened house in the first place.

"I'm sure," Massie mumbled.

"'Kay. I'll count us in." Alicia swept her jet black locks into a high pony. "Ah-five, ah-six, ah-sev-uhn, EIGHT!"

The girls giggle-squealed as they flipped over their totes, emptying mountains of sweets onto the heads of their sleeping bags.

"This has got to be the most candy anyone's ever gotten on Halloween ehhhhh-ver." Kristen's sapphire eyes glinted. She dug her hands into the pile, lifted the candy, and let it slip through her fingers. "Definitely my personal best."

"Same." Looking down at the colorful spread of gummies, candy bars, sours, and toffee in front of her, Claire felt an anticipatory sugar rush.

"News flash." Dylan pinch-lifted the corner of a cellophane-wrapped bar. "Protein bars do nawt qualify as candy."

"Mine!" Kristen and Alicia slapped the carpet with their palms.

Dylan grinned mischievously. "Make me an offer I can't ref—"

". . . GROUNDBREAKING FINNISH RESEARCH FROM THE HELSINKI EDUCATION AND RESEARCH TRUST, OR H.E.A.R.T., HAS PROVEN THAT CONFIDENCE IS THE NUMBER ONE MOST ATTRACTIVE QUALITY IN A PROSPECTIVE MATE," bleated a woman's voice from the surround-sound speakers in Massie's room.

"Ahhhhhhhhhhh!" Claire, Dylan, Kristen, and Alicia plugged their ears. Claire's head snapped toward Massie's bed, where the alpha was lying in the center of her fluffy purple duvet. Hands glued to her side, the tips of her fangs peeking out, she looked like a sleeping trampire in a down-filled coffin. Claire's heart sank.

Dylan leapt up, hopping over Claire and Kristen to get to Massie's nightstand. She yanked the iPod off the dock and tossed it on the bed next to Massie. The room fell silent again.

"Thank Gawd." Alicia reached for a sour gum ball.

Massie bolted upright like she'd been brought back from the dead. "Dylan!" she huffed. "That's my confidence CD!"

"Yeah, we heard." Dylan wince-rubbed her ears. "And so did everybody in HELSIIINKIIIII." She lowered her voice an octave, mimicking the sound of the narrator's voice.

The PC burst out laughing, reaching into their piles and lobbing handfuls of treats across the room in Massie's direction. Claire crossed her fingers at her side, waiting for Massie's reaction.

Dodging a flurry of foil-wrapped Hershey's bullets, Massie cracked a smile. "Shut up." She slid off her bed and followed Dylan to the circle.

Claire relaxed a little and reached for a giant baggie of gummies Cam had slipped into her bag after the last house of the night. She loved that with Cam, she didn't have to worry about orange ninth-graders at Halloween parties, or whether he thought trick-or-treating was lame. They were on exactly the same page.

"Ehmagawd, Josh just posted Twitterpics from tonight!" Alicia announced, beaming down at her cell.

"Twitt-er-treat!" Claire giggled.

Massie groaned, scratching behind her sleeping puppy's ears.

"And he tweeted that we looked ah-mazing in our costumes," Alicia added. "I swear, that boy is such a twirt."

"Twirt?" Claire repeated, lowering a sugar crystal–coated gummy onto her tongue.

"Twitter flirt," Kristen clarified, launching chocolate-covered pistachios across the circle into Dylan's open mouth.

Claire, Kristen, and Dylan circled around Alicia to get a better look. Alicia scrolled through shots of Josh and Cam making skeletons hump jack-o'-lanterns, Dempsey dodging bloody eyeballs, and Derrington stuffing Twizzlers up his nose.

"There aren't even any pictures of us!" Kristen complained. "Just a bunch of Dempsey in his mom's skirt!"

"I still can't believe my dress was too big on Josh." Alicia snapped the waistband on her gray silk tap shorts, sucking in her dance-sculpted abs.

"I can't believe Josh actually wore that dress in public," Massie added, rolling her eyes.

"And I can't believe Derrington fit a whole bag of Hershey Kisses in his mouth at once," Dylan jumped in. Claire couldn't tell if she was grossed out or impressed.

Suddenly, she realized the other girls were all focused on her, like they were waiting for something.

"Well?" Massie said impatiently, leveling her kohl-smudged gaze at Claire. Even Bean opened her left eye to stare at Claire.

"Ummmm." Claire balanced the bag of gummies on the thigh of her paisley-print Old Navy pajama pants. Why did she suddenly feel the urge to defend Cam to her friends? To start listing everything that was amazing about him, from the way he looked at her with his one green eye and one blue eye in the second before they lip-kissed, to the way he always offered her his Tomahawks warm-up jacket when she got cold? "I thought all that stuff was kinda funny." *And an hour ago, so did you,* she wanted to add.

"You would." Massie nodded knowingly.

"What's that supposed to mean?" Claire felt a knot starting to form in her stomach.

"It means that eighth-grade crushes are beyond immature," Massie explained slowly, in the same voice she used when she got impatient with Bean or the salesgirls at Neiman's. "But you wouldn't get that, 'cause you've never upgraded."

"Upgraded?" Claire repeated, digging her toes into the slick fabric of her sleeping bag.

"Waitaminute." Alicia loosened her ponytail to release face-framing layers from the grip of her rubber band. She did it whenever she wanted to look older. "Upgrade. Meaning, crushing on boys in the grade above us?"

"Ehhhh-xactly." Massie nodded. "Boys in ninth are so much more ma-toor." She slipped her Glossip Girl Candy Corn gloss from the pocket of her robe and slathered on a shiny coat. "Which is why I think we should all upgrade our crushes," she finished dramatically.

Alicia nibbled her lower lip.

Kristen cracked her knuckles.

Dylan unwrapped a toffee bar and crammed half into her mouth.

And Claire's heart bottomed out faster than the Freefall at Six Flags. Was Massie seriously serious? Claire dug into her gummy stash and crammed a handful into her mouth, waiting for the other girls to jump in and defend their crushes.

The sugar soothed her, but only for a second. Massie was slipping back into her old, controlling ways, which was exactly what had broken up the PC just weeks ago. Claire didn't know if she could survive another Pretty Committee breakup. She didn't know if she wanted to. Managing her friends' fights was getting to be more than she could handle. And she certainly wasn't going to ditch Cam just because Massie was having crush trust issues.

She glanced up expectantly, almost afraid of the girls' reactions.

Alicia took a deep breath. "Love it." She air-clapped, her brown eyes sparkling with interest.

"Ehmagawd, me too," Dylan sigh-added, looking relieved.

"Same!" Kristen piped up.

WHAT? Claire pressed her palms into the floor to steady herself, feeling like Massie's bedroom had suddenly been transformed into a giant Tilt-A-Whirl. Had the sugar overload made her friends completely insane? Was it the full moon? She yanked at the tiny hole in the knee of her pajama pants, making it bigger and bigger. It felt like the hole forming in her stomach.

"You're just gonna ditch your crushes? Just like that?" she squeaked, avoiding Massie's self-satisfied stare.

Alicia stretched out her legs in front of her, pointing and flexing her polished toes. "Maybe I want a crush who doesn't wear a dress size smaller than me," she said lightly. "Boys in ninth don't dress up for Halloween, so I wouldn't have to worry about that."

"Plus, older guys talk about more than just soccer," Kristen added.

"But you love soccer!" Claire protested, wanting to take her friends by the shoulders and shake them.

"I love other things too," Kristen said defensively. "Not that Dempsey knows that. He thinks I'm just one of the dudes."

Claire could feel heat rushing to her cheeks. She took a deep breath, trying to slow her racing heart.

"What about you?" she asked Dylan.

Dylan swallowed. "I heart Derrington," she said simply.

Claire breathed a sigh of relief.

"But more as, like, a younger brother than a crush, you know?" Dylan finished.

"I toe-dally know what you mean," Alicia jumped in. "Josh is two-point-five months younger than me, and it's starting to show." She wound her locks into a messy bun and held them in place with a Pixy Stix.

"He's the same age we are!" Claire flopped onto her stomach, wanting to scream and yell and cry. But mostly she just wanted to throttle Massie. "Just last week you guys were all in love with your crushes! What happened?"

"They grew up," Massie said, looking pleased with herself.

"These crushes were fun and all, but it's time to move awn," Kristen said earnestly. "Plus, they don't go to OCD anymore, so . . ."

Dylan turned toward Claire. "How're you gonna tell Cam?" she asked, wiping a chocolate smudge from her cheek with the edge of her cami.

Suddenly, Claire felt sick. The kind of sick she felt after washing down an entire bag of gummies with a cherry slushy from the mall.

"I'm not gonna tell him," she said firmly.

Alicia flashed a devilish grin. "So you're gonna cheat on him?" she asked, leaning forward.

"No!" Claire screeched, wiping her damp bangs from her

sweat-beaded forehead. "I'm not dumping him, and I'm not cheating on him. And I'm definitely not getting a ninth-grade crush!"

"Ninth is the new black, Claire," Massie snapped, finger-combing her ends. "Not that I'd expect you to get that."

Claire was too exhausted and confused to argue. The gummies in her stomach were charging toward her throat.

Stunned into silence, she watched as the rest of the girls chattered excitedly about their nonexistent new crushes. Claire picked at the hole in her pj's. If the girls moved on to ninth, where would that leave Claire? They'd be going to ninth-grade parties, doing ninth-grade things like over-bronzing and underdressing for movie night. And Claire and Cam would be tossed aside like the outfits in Merri-Lee Marvil's closet. She'd be expired.

Or even worse, immature.

Early the next morning, the Pretty Committee stood single file outside Bark Jacobs boutique in downtown Westchester, waiting for the clock on Massie's iPhone to buzz ten a.m. Massie stood at the head of the line, carefully inspecting her shimmering reflection in the boutique's freshly Windexed glass double doors.

She'd gotten up a full hour before the rest of the girls to give herself plenty of prep time. Just because she hadn't made the best impression on Landon last night didn't mean she couldn't impress his mom this morning. In crisp dark denim, an ivory cashmere tee, and her new French Connection cropped boyfriend jacket, Massie was the poster child for casual chic. Plus, her velvet Miu Miu ballet flats were leather-free, which practically screamed *I would never hurt an animal on purpose! Even for fashion!*

At exactly ten a.m., Massie swiveled to face the Pretty Committee, like a general addressing her troops before battle.

"Remember, if we don't find a get-well gift for Bark that makes Landon and Bark forgive me ay-sap, the entire upgrade could be in jeopardy." Her heart skipped a beat at the terrifying thought.

At the head of the line, Alicia gasped, the color draining from her Nars-dusted cheeks. "Opposite of acceptable."

Massie nodded. "Just think of Landon Crane as your VIP pass to the exclusive world of ninth-grade—"

From her place at the back of the line, Claire cough-muttered something unintelligible.

Massie froze. Ever since she'd debuted the upgrade idea the night before, Claire had been wrinkling her nose like Massie was week-old sushi.

"Comments?" Massie leaned to the side and arched her eyebrow in Claire's general direction. She would have made eye contact if Dylan's sugar-matted bedhead 'fro weren't blocking her view.

Kristen chewed her Essie Ew No You Didn't–polished thumbnail. Alicia smoothed down her Ralph Lauren wool skirt. Claire's Kedded foot tapped behind Dylan's riding boots.

"Perf." Massie whirled back around and gripped the brushed-silver, dog bone–shaped door handles. A blast of warm, gingerbread-scented air whooshed past her as a tiny *yip* chime-announced the Pretty Committee's arrival.

The last time Massie had walked through these doors, she'd been followed by the cast of vapid, b-for-beta-list actresses she'd hired to be part of her new group, Massie and Crew, to make the Soul-M8s jealous. Entering now with the Pretty Committee made Bark Jacobs seem fresh and new, like she was discovering it for the first time. The large gold paw prints that crisscrossed the slick marble floor on the way to the doggie dressing rooms seemed shinier. The glass display cases that boasted pet-size designer bags, accessories, and jewelry seemed sleeker. And the racks of canine couture around the boutique's perimeter seemed ten times more chic.

"Welcome to Bark Jacobs!" chirped a voice Massie didn't recognize. A megawatt blonde in an all-black ensemble emerged from the back of the store, a pewter dog bowl filled with dog treats in her hands. A bony Italian greyhound puppy in a sage-green felt cloche trotted behind her. "Are you looking for something in particular, or—"

"Celia Crane?" Massie scanned the empty, brightly lit boutique for Landon's mom. What was the point of getting Bark a get-well gift, if Celia couldn't see just how much of a pup-lanthropist Massie was? And if Celia just so happened to pass the information along to Landon, well . . .

The salesgirl's face fell. "She's not working today," she informed the PC in hushed tones, hugging the bowl of dog food to her chest like it was a baby. "Family emergency. Her grand-dog was in a lethal accident last night, and she had to go with her son to the vet this morning."

The greyhound let out a low whimper and buried his snout in his paws. Alicia giggle-gasped.

Massie elbowed her in the ribs. "That's horrible," she said, pity-widening her eyes. She applied a quick layer of Strawberry Fro-Yo Glossip Girl to still her quavering lips. Had Bark taken a turn for the worse? Had her stiletto maimed him for life? Maybe he'd gotten an infection and amputation was the only way to save him. Ehmagawd, would Bark need a bionic paw?

"What happened?" Kristen retied her chunky turquoise scarf around her neck.

"Is Ba—I mean, the dog gonna be okay?" Claire finger-tossed her sleep-matted bangs.

"Too soon to tell." The salesgirl lowered the dog bowl onto the glass case and blinked at the ceiling, her eyes bright with tears.

Massie swallowed back a wave of guilt-nausea.

Yip! Yip! The door chime signaled another customer.

"Just let me know if you need anything." The salesgirl dabbed at her eyes with her sleeve. "And help yourselves to a gingerbread paw," she added, tapping the dog bowl with a polished index finger. "They're from PureBread, Celia's new line of organic treats for pets and humans." She hurried past the PC to the front of the store.

"Ew." Alicia wrinkled her nose.

"Yum," Dylan said at the same time, her hand shooting into the dog bowl.

"Cam loves gingerbread," Claire sighed morosely.

"Lethal?" Massie repeated, leaning against the cool glass case for support.

"She's ahbviously exaggerating, Mass." Alicia examined a tiny Hermès scarf on a velvet-lined tray. "Do Landon's single guy friends have dogs too? Maybe I should get this."

"I need to prove what an animal lover I am." Massie pinched a gingerbread paw and nibbled at the rounded edge. But instead of soothing her, the spicy-sweet treat made her stomach lurch. "Remember when Hayden got arrested for trying to save the seals?"

"Wasn't it dolphins?" Kristen corrected her.

Massie ignored her. "And did I nawt wear my CLUB SODA, NOT SEALS shirt to the gym the next day, to show support?"

"Plus, I saw four girls from sixth wearing the same shirt at school the next day," Alicia said. "You practically started a movement."

"Given." Massie nodded. "Except Landon doesn't know that."

"So show him." Kristen clapped. She headed for the wall of puppy footwear on the other side of the store, her heels clacking with determination. "How about some puppy Pumas?" she called, lifting a miniscule pair of metallic street sneakers over her head.

Alicia rolled her eyes. "He can't walk, re-mem-ber?"

Dylan grabbed another handful of gingerbread paws and followed Kristen. "At least that way he can kick up his paws in style," she grinned over her shoulder.

Massie shook her head, her chestnut locks fanning around her shoulders like a silky pashmina. "Nawt good enough."

"Um . . . what about a new doggie bed?" Claire sank onto a pile of giant silk pet pillows at Massie's feet. "You could get it monogrammed or something. And since Bark's gonna need bed rest . . ."

"Better," Massie admitted. "But still not it." She tapped the glass with her index finger, letting her eyes travel from the selection of jeweled kitty chokers to the tiny puppy Ray-Bans. *No, no, and no.*

"Got it!" Dylan squealed from somewhere in the back of

the store. She barreled past the footwear display, her tousled tresses flapping wildly behind her. She was cradling a small cardboard box in her arms like it was a rare Nancy Gonzalez origami tote. "It's called the Mutt Monitor. It's like a baby monitor, but for pets. That way Landon can keep an eye on Bark while he recovers." Breathless, she held up the box for Massie to see.

The idea was actually perfect enough that Massie wished it had been hers. There was only one problem.

"He can't have a monitor at school though," she pointed out. "We need something where he can check on the puppy during the day without getting caught."

"What about the SnoopDawg 2000?" The peppy salesgirl appeared out of nowhere, sliding behind the glass case and producing a small silver key from her pocket. She inserted it into the lock and slid open the case. "It's the newest edition of our original SnoopDawg camera charm." Her fingers flew over the charms until she found the tiny silver bone-shaped charm, and she lifted it for Massie to see. "It allows the tech-savvy animal lover to track pets in real time on the Snoop-Dawg Web site. Plus, it's iPhone compatible."

"Perfect!" Massie air-clapped.

The salesgirl nodded. "And the camera inside has a rotating lens, so you get a 360-degree view."

Massie quickly side-glanced at Bean, whose own Snoop-Dawg charm had turned to her furry chest again.

"It's the only one of its kind on the market." The charm gleamed and glinted in the golden boutique lighting.

"Upgrade!" Alicia announced happily.

Kristen skipped up behind Massie, slapping her playfully on the shoulder. "Does Landon have any friends that play varsity soccer?" she asked quietly, a devilish grin on her face. "I'm so over J.V."

Claire sighed, pushing herself to her feet. "Isn't it a little quick to be scouting soccer players?" she asked, clearly annoyed.

"Of course, it's slightly more expensive than the original . . ." the salesgirl continued.

"I'll take it." Massie reached for her clutch, relief washing over her like a triple spritz of cooling Evian facial mist. The SnoopDawg 2000 was the perfect way to show Landon how much she cared about Bark. She grinned at her friends.

The upgrade was *awn*.

"It's like . . ." Claire leaned forward in Layne's corduroy papasan chair and wrapped herself in a rainbow-colored mohair throw, searching for the perfect metaphor to convey just how casually her friends were treating the idea of ditching their crushes. "It's like the boys are basic Prada hobos they ordered off Saks last season. And then this season's trendy Proenza Schouler totes came out and they thought, 'Hey! These bags are waaaaay more mature.' And so now they want to exchange the hobos for the totes, which is the worst idea ever, because the hobos are cute and sweet and funny and go with everything!" Claire surfaced for air, refocusing her gaze on Layne, who was sitting cross-legged on her glow-in-the-dark duvet.

Layne's jaw dropped. "English, please."

Claire collapsed back into the cushion, staring up at the plastic stars glued to Layne's ceiling. Her head was throbbing, and this time she couldn't blame it on the combination beef jerky–mothball–vanilla Glade smell of Layne's bedroom. "It's like their old crushes are vintage Salvation Army finds and now they want shiny new ninth-grade crushes from Macy's."

"Ohhhhhhhhh." Layne nodded. "Got it."

Claire whipped the mohair throw onto the floor in despair.

It landed with a loud crumple on top of an empty jumbo bag of Funions. Layne's bedroom floor was strewn with cut-up issues of *National Geographic, Entertainment Weekly,* and *Martha Stewart Living.* Three colorful bolts of fabric were balled in the corner, and a hot glue gun had leaked what looked like a glittery blue booger onto Layne's cream throw carpet. But Layne's room felt neat and ordered, compared to the swirling chaos of Claire's brain.

"Does this include Kristen?" Layne drummed her fingers together, her brows wiggling over smudges of bright purple shadow. In the neon glow of the red lava lamp on her bedside table, she looked like an exchange student from hell. "Because if Dempsey's available—"

Claire glare-silenced her. "Layne."

"Sorry. Refocusing. So what does Cam say?"

"Nothing. I haven't told him yet." Claire sighed miserably. All day, Cam had been texting about the post–trick-or-treating fun he and the boys had had at Josh's. About how he'd eaten so much candy corn that his skin was starting to look orange, and how Dempsey and Josh had toilet-papered Derrington after he'd fallen asleep. But what was Claire supposed to text back? *Don't tell Alicia or Dylan—they think mummies are im*mum*ture?*

"The guys don't deserve this!" she said, the panic in her stomach hardening into anger.

"Yeah!" Layne nodded, bolting upright and pumping her fist into the air. Each of her fingernails was painted a different neon color. "What did Dempsey ever do to Kristen?"

"Nothing!" Amped-up energy rushed to Claire's head like sparkling cider bubbles to the top of a champagne flute. "So Derrington wiggles his butt and Josh likes to dress in drag. It's funny, right?"

"Right!" Layne leapt up on her bed, bouncing on her mattress. "Well, it's actually not really my thing, but whatever!"

"We have to do something!" Claire decided, jumping from the papasan chair to the floor. She landed on a pile of Layne's dirty clothes and hopped over the fabric bolts, the glue gun, and an open jewelry box filled with tiny fake jewels to get to the bed.

"We have to do the right thing!" Layne declared, crouching down to pull Claire up. The girls gripped each other's hands, bouncing up and down on the bed.

"Because eighth-grade crushes everywhere need our help!" Claire barked, her bangs flop-fanning her forehead.

"It's up to us to save the males," Layne declared.

"Yesssssssssssss!" Claire huffed, feeling all the built-up tension from the night before slowly drain from her body as she sailed in the air, the crooked Broadway show posters on Layne's wall spinning in a blur around her. "What's our first mission?"

"This!" Layne stuck out her bare foot, tripping Claire and sending both girls flopping onto the mattress in a heap of giggles.

Out of breath, Claire rolled onto her back. "We do . . . actually . . . need a . . . plan," she heaved. "Something to make the girls think ninth-grade crushes are a terrible idea."

Layne waved her away. "I'll come up with something. Gimme a second."

The girls stared at the greenish glow-in-the-dark universe overhead, lapsing into silence. Her head a little clearer, Claire tried to brainstorm ways to convince Massie that eighth-grade boys were ten times better than ninth-grade ones. But instead of a plan, her brain drifted to images of Cam. Cam on his bike, coasting down Massie's driveway, his blue eye bluer than the sky while his green one made the manicured grass look faded and dull. Cam in his ump-pire costume, which he'd picked to go with her trampire costume so the whole world would know they were crushes. Cam on the soccer field, easing the soccer ball effortlessly toward the net. Cam with a giant baggie of gummies, slipping them into Claire's candy ba—

"Got it!" Layne slapped the duvet with her palm, jolting Claire out of her daydream. "And it's totally inspired."

"What?" Claire flopped onto her stomach and kicked off her giraffe-printed Keds. They landed with a thump on the bedroom floor.

Layne shook her head. "It's top secret," she said mysteriously.

"Layne!" Claire swatted her with one of the puff-painted pillows strewn across Layne's bed. "It can't be top secret from me! This mission was my idea in the first place!"

"The less you know, the better." Layne grinned, obviously enjoying herself. "Meet in the café Tuesday at oh-twelve-hundred hours. Don't be late."

Claire rolled her eyes. "Are you sure this is gonna work?"

"Please. Have I ever steered you wrong?" Layne turned to face Claire, her frizzy brown flyaways tumbling over her eyes. "Trust me, dahhhh-ling." She wiggled her pinky finger.

Claire latched her pinky with Layne's and shook on it. She wanted to believe Layne had the perfect, foolproof plan. That by lunchtime on Tuesday, Massie and the girls would rediscover their crushes and fall in love with them all over again, like the boys were rare vintage handbags that seemed even better the second time around.

Eighth-grade crushes might be endangered—like blue whales or the African wild ass—but if Claire had anything to say about it, they were nawt going to become extinct.

"Second entrance on the right, Isaac," Massie instructed the Block family driver from the backseat of the Range Rover. Bean was perched on her lap, peering warily out the tinted window at the cracked brick ADD sign at the school's rusted metal gate.

"Got it." Isaac beamed into the rearview mirror, looking prouder than Massie had been on the day of Bean's graduation from puppy obedience school. The Range Rover slowed and turned onto a paved road that was faded and lined with yellowed crabgrass. "You know, I'm glad you girls are considering public school for next year. It shows real maturity to broaden your horizons like this."

Across from Massie, Alicia, Kristen, Claire, and Dylan gripped their black leather armrests at the very idea.

Massie swallowed a laugh. Going public was like flying coach—fine for a short flight, but for four years of high school? Absolutely nawt. But Isaac would never have agreed to the stakeout if he knew her real motives. For that matter, neither would the Pretty Committee; they thought there were there to pick out new crushes. Massie admitting that she wanted to spy on Landon would be like Demi Moore owning up to her airbrush job on the cover of *W*: It would totally ruin appearances, and secretly, everybody probably already knew anyway.

"How's my hair?" Dylan speed-combed her locks. "I want it to look perfect for all the ninth-grade hawt—"

Alicia pinched Dylan's thigh.

"FOR WHEN WE MEET THE PRINCIPAL," Dylan finished loudly. "YOU KNOW WHAT THEY SAY. YOU NEVER HAVE A SECOND CHANCE TO MAKE A FIRST—"

Massie pressed the silver armrest button that activated the tinted divider between the front and back seats, creating a soundproof barrier between Isaac and the PC.

"Sorry." Dylan's cheeks turned pink.

Massie wished her seat came equipped with its own personal divider, so she could close herself off from the rest of the Range Rover and do all the things she was dying to do but wouldn't be caught dead doing. Like check her iPhone again for a text, Twitter post, or voice mail from Landon, thanking her for the SnoopDawg 2000, which she'd had messengered to him. Or click to her newly formed Facebook group, EATA (Ethical Animal Treatment by Alphas) to see if Landon had joined in the last seven minutes.

Why hadn't he called? Did he seriously prefer over-bronzed ninth-grade girls who wore minis to movie night and hadn't trick-or-treated in years? Massie had texted over the weekend to make sure he knew that for her, Halloween was all about the fashion, not the candy. But what if he thought she was immature? Sure, every magazine worth its weight in ad sales said men prefer younger women, but what if *Cosmo* had been misleading her all this time?

Massie pressed her hands into the soft leather seat, her entire body buzzing with nervous energy. Or was that just the Range Rover, navigating the crumbling, cracked concrete of the ADD driveway?

"Ehhhhhhhhmagaaaaaaaawd," Alicia's voice trembled as Isaac shifted into four-wheel drive. The Kevyn Aucoin liner she'd been holding to her lips shook violently, giving her a jagged, plum-colored mustache.

"Hahaaaaaaaaa," Kristen giggled.

Claire crossed her arms over her white Inhabit henley and stared out the window. "It's not *that* bad."

Massie ignored her and popped the mix she'd made last night into the CD player built into the leather bench. Immediately, Avril Lavigne's "I Can Do Better" blasted from the speakers. All Claire needed was a little taste of an upgrade, and she'd come around. She always did. In fact, Massie had been upgrading Claire since the second she'd moved to Westchester from Orlandull. If it weren't for Massie, Claire's closet would still be filled with puff-painted Keds and tacky baby tees that read things like THIS SHIRT IS BANANAS or NERD FETISH.

"Positions," Massie announced as Isaac pulled around the front circle. She retied the sash on her See by Chloé camo dress.

Everyone except for Claire reached into their handbags, producing the sleek silver binoculars Massie had brought for the stakeout.

"How long is this gonna take?" Claire sighed, checking her Baby G-Shock watch. "I'm supposed to ride bikes with Cam later, but I have to finish my homework first."

"This is your homework." Massie pressed the cool metal to her eyes, examining a group of baggy-jeaned boys playing Hacky Sack in front of the flag-less flagpole. Their hems were muddy and torn, and they were wearing Simples. *Ew.* "Only instead of an A, you get a C."

"C?"

"A crush," Massie said, clarifying the obvious.

"I told you," Claire huffed. "I don't want a—"

"Ehmaspandex!" Dylan pointed out the window.

"Where?" Kristen swung her binoculars toward the other side of the Range Rover. A girl with Pippi braids wearing a Syracuse hoodie over hot-pink stretch pants skipped over to a waiting blue Honda.

"Dylan!" Alicia whisper-hissed. "Don't point. You'll scare it away."

Dylan stuck her tongue out at Alicia, then reached into the crumpled bag of M&Ms in her lap. "It's like a whole different world out here."

"I feel like we're on safari." Alicia adjusted the sleeves on her army-green Twenty8Twelve fitted blazer. "Watching the poor and fashion-challenged in their natural habitat."

Kristen sank back into the leather bench. "Don't say 'safari,'" she groaned. "If I hear one more 'This one time? In Africa?' story, I'm going to import a lion to eat him."

Massie leaned toward the front seat and lowered the

divider. "Just park here," she called over the sound of the music. "We're going to sit for a minute and check out the scene."

Isaac nodded and pulled over to the curb, next to the free-standing ADD cafeteria.

"At least Dempsey doesn't keep losing bets," Dylan grumbled. "Josh bet Derrington he couldn't beat him three times in a row at Soccer FIFA 09."

"And?" Kristen grinned.

Dylan's chin dropped to her green Free People cardigan. "Now he has to wear his clothes backward till Christmas."

Massie fought back a smile. Landon may not have returned her texts, but at least he put his clothes on the right way.

The jostling stopped when Isaac shifted the Range Rover into PARK, but Massie's insides didn't stop vibrating. She dipped her hand into her purse and tapped her Nars bronzing powder with her fingertips, sneaking a quick cheek-swipe when the other girls weren't looking.

The creaking clang of the final bell echoed across campus, and the building's main doors swung open.

"Time to upgrade, girls," she announced as herds of ADD kids spilled onto the front lawn.

The girls bolted upright, ready for action.

"Make sure all the kids are carrying lots of books," Massie said loudly enough for Isaac to hear, as the girls all pulled out their cells. "We want to make sure high school challenges us to reach our full potential."

Massie: Translation: if u see any hawt boys, take their pics. I'll have Landon ID later. ☺
Alicia: Done.
Kristen: Done.
Dylan: And done.

Claire just pulled her math textbook out of her Roxy backpack.

Massie was about to lecture her when the doors of the main building flew open, and out stepped a boy in perfectly faded Genetic Denim jeans and a gray Black Hearts Brigade T-shirt. His inky black curls glinted in the bright November sun, his blue eyes shone, and the messenger bag slung over his shoulder was definitely designer—Prada? Dolce? Bean *yip*-licked the window.

"Target locked on and acquired," Massie said, as Miles, Ace, and a bunch of other guys crowded around Landon, talking and laugh-punching one another.

"Ehmagawd!" Dylan and Alicia squealed.

"Who's *that*?" Kristen pointed to a girl making her way up to Landon. Her waist-long dreadlocks were dyed half red and half yellow, and she wore a gray Levi's denim jacket, black bike shorts, and red Converse sneakers.

"My eyes!" Alicia jammed on her sunglasses at the sight of the offending outfit.

"Shhh!" Massie pressed her nose against the window, watching as the Ronald McDonald look-alike handed something to Landon. He smiled, the same way he used to smile at Massie the week before. She dropped her silver binoculars in her lap.

"Who is that?" Even Claire slammed her textbook shut and stared.

"Probs just a friend," Massie said, her mouth suddenly dry. She resisted the urge to grab McDreads by the hair and sling-hurl her across the potholed lawn. "Older guys usually have a lot of girl friends, but they're not, like, girlfriends."

Landon pulled out his phone and asked the girl something. Ehmagawd. Probably her phone number.

The PC were silent, pity filling their faces. The already taut sash on Massie's camo dress was starting to feel like a boa constrictor, squeezing all the confidence from her body. She should've known Landon would ditch her like all the other guys she'd ever crush—

Ping.

Landon: Just got the SnoopDawg 2000. Awesome! Thx!

And just like that, the sash felt like a warm hug reminding her that miracles happen every day.

Massie: No prob. Thought u could use it to check on Bark while he recovers . . .

She neglected to add the best part about the gift: She could use the SnoopDawg 2000 to keep a close eye on Landon.

Landon: Totally. Where r u? Want 2 get the dogs 2gether?

"Isaac!" Massie gripped her cell for dear life. "We've gotta get home! Now."

Isaac turned around in his seat, looking confused. "But what about your campus tou—"

"Canceled!" Panic twisted in her stomach like a carb-loaded, oversalted mall pretzel. Every second the Range Rover stayed parked in the ADD lot was another second she could get busted for being a crush chaser.

The PC collapsed back in their seats as Isaac peeled out of the parking lot, muttering something under his breath.

When the Range Rover was safely out of Landon's line of sight, Massie texted back, allowing herself to sneak a tiny breath of relief.

Massie: Play-d8 sounds gr8. Plans 2day tho. Friday?
Landon: Def. Where?
Massie: My house. The spa. Bark can get in the jacuzzi. The heat is gr8 4 pain.
Landon: Perfect. Bark will be psyched. Me too. ☺

"Spill!" Alicia begged, leaning forward.

Even Claire looked curious.

"He'scomingtothespaFridayafterschool!" Adrenaline pulsed through Massie's veins faster than her fingers could text. She'd just invited a Ninth. Grade. Boy. To her Jacuzzi.

"Tell him to bring his friends!" Dylan bounced up and down in her seat.

"'Kay!" Massie bounced back.

Massie: Oops! 4got I already told the Pretty Committee they could spa. Bring ur friends!
Landon: U sure?
Massie: So sure I'm raising my hands!
Landon: ????

"Done and done." Massie tossed her phone back into her bag, too worn out to text-explain the deodorant joke. Beads of sweat formed at her temples, and she sank back into the leather bench and closed her eyes. Text-managing her own love life, not to mention her friends', was exhausting.

"Yaaaaay!" Dylan, Alicia, and Kristen shouted. Dylan reached over and pressed the PLAY button on Massie's mix. Lady GaGa's "Love Game" came pumping through the sound system.

When Massie opened her eyes again, Claire was glaring at her. Her face was frozen in a Kristin Stewart–like grimace. But Massie refused to let Claire ruin her fun. The Pretty Committee were ready to upgrade.

Even if Claire was being a total downer.

Claire's denim-covered knees bounced uncontrollably underneath Table 18, making the tall stacks of *Seventeen*, *Vogue* (regular and *España*), and *In Style* on its surface quiver like a minor earthquake had struck the New Green Café.

"Claire." Massie slapped her palm on the stack in front of her, pinning a scantily clad Sienna Miller to the bamboo table. "Are you Julianne Hough?"

"No." Claire reached for her gummy stash to calm her nerves, but the sugar-smudged baggie in her lap was empty.

"Then quit shaking it." The rest of the PC snorted at the pages of their style bibles while Massie swiped the latest issue of *Vogue* from Alicia's pile. She flipped to the middle. "If I get Jakkob to do blunt bangs, do you think I'd look fifteen?" she mused into the glossy pages. "Or, like, eleven?"

"Could go either way," Alicia mused, side-glancing at Claire's bangs.

Dylan nodded, taking a long swig of her Blue Bubble Gum Jones Soda. "Risky."

"Ah-greed," Massie decided, tossing her side bangs past her decidedly bronzed cheekbones.

Claire's eyes traveled nervously back and forth between the mini vegetable gardens on her left and the Borba-stocked stagecoach on her right. Olivia Ryan was giggling with Kori, Strawberry, and Meena at Table 4. Seventh-graders jostled between the bamboo tables, carrying trays of teriyaki tofu, steaming bowls of black bean chili loaded with soy cheese, and plates of crispy veggie samosas. But instead of soothing her, the warm, spicy aromas that filled the café were starting to make her sweat. Where was Layne? According to the clock over the frosted glass doors, she was a full four minutes late. Which meant that Operation Save the Males was not off to a good start.

After yesterday's trip to ADD, Claire had to accept the truth: Unless she took action immediately, the PC would be spa-partying with a bunch of older guys by Friday. Hot tubs, dramatic breakups, strange new crushes: It would be like the Blocks' spa had been transformed into the set of *The Real World: Westchester*. Starting in . . .

Claire checked the clock again.

"Three days and six hours." Massie slapped her magazine closed, prompting the rest of the girls to do the same. "That's how long we have till Landon and your new crushes show up at the spa."

Alicia re-glossed.

Dylan sucked in her cheeks.

Kristen stretched her triceps.

And Claire gulped.

"Which means we're running out of time to update our looks so they're ninth-worthy." Massie yanked at the hem of her eggplant-colored Design History sweater. "WHICH means all changes have to be approved by the end of lunch."

"Lunch?" Dylan moaned, scavenging the table for food. But every square inch was covered with style mags.

"It's a figure of speech." Massie said.

"Oh." Dylan leaned back in her chair, looking weak.

"Now remember," Massie instructed the PC. "Nothing drastic. We're just going for a look that's us, only better. And a year older." She paused, glancing at Claire's black Gap turtleneck. "Or three. Whatevs."

Claire rolled her eyes, sneaking another look at the clock. Now Layne was seven minutes late.

"I'll start." Alicia lifted an issue of *People* from her pile, opening to a dog-eared page that featured a spread on the cast of *Gossip Girl*. "I'm going Jessica Szohr," she announced with a quick hair toss. "Shiny hair, boho fashion with a splash of Upper East Side." She paused, as if waiting for applause.

"Isn't that kind of your look already?" Kristen looked up from *Sports Illustrated*.

"Given," Alicia grinned. "Only this'll be sexier."

"What makes it sexier?" Dylan drained the last of her soda.

"A bikini."

"Now me," Kristen piped up, tightening her ponytail like she meant business. She had to prop herself up on her knees to see over the listing pile of *Sports Illustrated* and *Harper's Bazaar* in front of her. "It's all about Hayden." She held up a ripped *Heroes* promo ad. "I'm going with a laid-back surfer suit, natural makeup, and a center part." She yanked the elastic out of her hair, releasing her straight blond tresses to her shoulders. "It makes you look way more mature."

The girls' hands flew self-consciously to their side-parts.

Massie nodded. "Dylan?"

Dylan lurched forward in her seat. "Ummm . . . I think I'm doing Nicole Kidman?" She pawed frantically through the crinkled pages in front of her. "Her hair's looking really red these days."

The Pretty Committee all stared at her.

"The point is to look like we're nawt middle school," Massie elbow-nudged her. "Or middle age."

Dylan rolled her eyes. "Fine. Taylor Swift?"

"Good." Massie straightened up, suddenly looking serious. "Now me." She released her iPhone to the table and nodded at the neat row of pages arranged in front of her. Sunlight from the large glass windows in the New Green Café illuminated reflective shots of celebrities from Jessica (Biel, not Simpson) to Angelina. Different body parts, accessories, and wardrobe pieces had been circled with Massie's Smashbox Palm Beach lip liner, with notations like ♥ THE HEMLINE! and SMUDGED LINER ADDS 6 MONTHS TO YOUNG-LOOKING EYES! scribbled in the margins. "I've been thinking about it, and I narrowed my look down to Leighton Meester, Camilla Belle, or Natalie Portman."

"So?" Dylan bounced in her seat. "What's it gonna be?"

The Pretty Committee leaned forwardly expectantly.

"None of the above," Massie said, swiping the pages from

the space in front of her like her bangle-covered forearm was a giant, Chanel-spritzed windshield wiper. "The look I'm going for is . . . Massie Block," she finished coyly. "If it's working, why change it?"

Just as Claire was about to roll her eyes, she caught a glimpse of Layne charging through the glass doors on the other side of the café. She was dressed in a black terry cloth track suit, a white puffy coat, and two army green scarves, and her face was bright red. Stage-winking at Claire, she held up an Evian bottle and doused herself with "sweat."

Claire bit the inside of her cheek to keep from laughing.

"Comin' through!" Layne bellowed, making a beeline for the Pretty Committee like she was a marathon runner and Table 18 was the finish line.

A pained looked settled over Massie's tanned face.

"You. Are. Not. Gonna. Buh. Lieve. This," Layne wheezed, doubling over the table.

Massie wrinkled her nose as two drops of Evian sweat dripped from Layne's nose onto Charlize Theron's thigh. "Layne, are you a decimal system?" she asked, scooting her chair a few inches to the left.

"No." Layne coughed, planting her wet forehead on a stack of *Us Weekly*s.

"Then why are you so Dewey?" Massie cracked.

"Point!" Alicia flip-tousled her hair for volume.

Layne whipped a thick black notebook from underneath her puffy coat and tossed it in the center of the table. It was covered in Fall Out Boy and Metro Station bumper stickers.

Claire crossed her fingers under the table as Massie eyed the worn notebook, clearly trying not to look curious.

"It's my brother's journal," Layne heaved, looking like she might give in to heatstroke at any second.

"Chris Abeley keeps a journal?" Massie looked impressed.

Layne bobbed her head up and down. "Anyhoo, I stole it this morning. And it's all about how dirty high school boys are and how they like to use middle school girls. Especially private school ones."

Dylan's jaw dropped. "For what?"

"You know," Layne said vaguely. "Dirty . . . stuff."

"Ewwwwwww." Alicia looked half grossed out, half curious.

"Are you serious?" Kristen bit her lower lip.

Claire pinched her thigh to keep from laughing.

Layne nodded. "And I'm pretty sure somebody found out I took the journal, 'cause I was definitely being followed on the way here. But I had to tell you guys, 'cause I know you've been hanging out with Landon and stuff." She glanced meaningfully at Massie.

"Landon's nawt dirty," Massie decided, although she looked uncertain. She reached into her hobo and pulled out a fresh tube of Glossip Girl, gripping it like it was a weapon.

"Oh yeah?" Layne challenged. "Then how come he gave Bean that charm collar with the camera in it?" She didn't skip a beat. "Probably so he can spy on you when you're changing and taking a shower and stuff."

Alicia gasped, crossing her arms over her C-cups. "Opposite of possible."

Layne shrugged. "Says you," she said, wiping her dripping forehead.

An uneasy silence settled over Table 18, making the sounds around them of clinking silverware, lunchtime gossip, and scraping bamboo chairs seem ten times louder than before. Claire side-glanced at Massie, who was speed-glossing with the ferocity of a snapping shark.

Claire relaxed back in her chair. It looked like *The Real World: Westchester* was being canceled before it even premiered. She resisted the urge to leap across the table and bear-hug Layne. The girl deserved an Oscar.

Suddenly, Massie reached across the table, grabbing the journal.

"Hey!" Layne lunged for the journal, but Massie held it out of her reach. "That's mi—I mean, my brother's!"

Massie flipped the notebook open to the last page, her amber eyes sliding back and forth. Seconds later, she slammed the open journal onto the table.

"'October 31st. Dear diary. Halloween is, like, the best holiday there is. Me and my ninth-grade friends can't wait to do all kinds of dirty stuff to all the eighth-grade OCD girls in trampy costumes. Especially the ones dressed like vampires.'"

Alicia gasped.

"'But not my awesome sister, Layne,'" Massie continued dryly.

Claire's stomach heaved. Suddenly, the warm sunlight beaming through the skylights felt like one of those overhead interrogation lights on *CSI*. Tiny beads of sweat formed underneath her bangs, threatening to drip pale rivers down her lightly bronzed forehead.

"'She's totally un-slutty. Actually she's, like, the coolest, most original—'" Massie stopped reading and held up the diary. The pages were covered in glitter-marker scrawl. "Could you be any more ahbv-ious?" She rolled her eyes. "This is a total fake."

"Layyyyne!" Kristen swatted Layne's puffy white arm with a rolled-up magazine.

Massie leveled her glowing amber eyes at Claire, like she could read her innermost thoughts. "Take your dia-ryuhhh and leave, Layne," she snapped, without shifting her gaze from Claire.

"Fine." Layne swiped the journal from Massie's grip, shoved back her chair, and apology-shrugged at Claire before stalking off in her puffy coat.

Claire clenched her jaw. Strike one. And now that Massie's scheme-dar was up, saving the males was going to take more than a doctored diary.

It was going to take a miracle.

Normally, the Zen-inspired dry section of the Blocks' spa was a stressed alpha's haven. The polished leather couches were inviting, the limestone fountain soothing, and the crackling fireplace comforting. If the feng shui space could talk, it would have whispered, *Relaaaaaaahhhhhhxx* to every visitor who stepped through the sliding wooden door.

Except for today. Today, the spa screamed, *Ehmagawd-ninth-gradeboysaregoingtobehereinTWODAYSandI'mnawteven-CLOSEtobeingready!*

With countless swimsuit rejects slung over the furniture, *Glamour* "Don't" lists papering the walls, and three Sephora bags full of waterproof makeup testers crowding the marble-topped coffee table, the spa was the opposite of relaxing. Not even Massie's *Sounds of the Rainforest* CD or Aquiesse Green Tea Pear candles were helping.

Massie stretched out in corpse pose, her tensed shoulders craving a deep-tissue massage. She and the Pretty Committee had scheduled a 9:00 p.m. conference call. She dialed Dylan on her iPhone and pressed SPEAKER.

"Time to get started," she barked, jamming a fresh pair of cucumber slices over her eyes. "Everybody there?"

"Present," Dylan mumbled over a mouthful of something crunchy.

"Tankinis are so sixth, right?" Alicia said.

"Ninety-niiiiiine, one-hundy!" Kristen groaned. "These boys better like six-packs."

Then the line went silent.

"Kuh-laire?" Massie prompted, rubbing her bare feet over the zebra-print ottoman. The prickly calf hair tickled her soles, making her giggle.

"Study date with Cam," Kristen said uncertainly. "She just IM'd."

"Shocker." These days, if it didn't involve Cam, Layne, eighth, or gummies, Claire wasn't interested. "First things first. Research."

Massie sat upright and reached for the lavender legal pad on the coffee table. The lukewarm cucumber slices plopped to the floor, and she nudged them under the couch with her big toe. She flipped to the survey she'd created, which she'd told her friends to send out to at least three older guys.

Directions:

Please complete this top secret, ah-nonymous government survey and text back to sender NO LATER than Friday at 12 p.m. Participants must be male and graduated from eighth. Anyone who does not meet these qualifications will be disqualified ay-sap. (This means Cam, Kuh-laire.)

1. If I were attending a hot spa party hosted by even hotter alphas, I'd . . .

   a) Snack on: _____
   (insert fave snacks here)

   b) Listen to: _____
   (insert fave tunes/bands here)

   c) Talk about: _____
   (insert fave conversation topics here)

   d) Play: _____
   (insert fave party/video games here)

2. Cover-ups: Marisa Miller—hawt or Ugly Betty—nawt?

3. One pieces: Sexy mama or grandmama?

4. Spa treatments for boys are . . .

   a) A must. How do you think Clooney's T-zone stays so taut?

   b) Not a deal breaker. But puh-lease, no girly-scented moisturizers.

   c) A reason to RVSP NO WAY.

"So tell me your results," Massie said. Hopefully, the other girls' data would be enough to guide the party planning, since she hadn't had time to find any acceptable older boys to survey. It wasn't that she didn't know any. It was just that the ones she did know were Landon Crane and Chris Abeley. And they already had her number in their phones, so what would be anonymous about that? "Results? D, you first."

The line went quiet again. The only sound in the spa was the croak of a rainforest tree frog and Dylan's chewing.

"I'm waaaaaiting." Massie dunked her hand in the nearest Sephora bag, retrieving a sample tube of Urban Decay Big Fatty waterproof mascara. Should she go for thickening or lengthening? Blue-black or kohl? Waterproof or resistant? The number of decisions she had to make before Friday was starting to feel overwhelming.

"Um . . . mymomtookawaymyphoneforgoingovermytextlimit."

"You got your cell taken away." Massie pinched a shimmering emerald Shoshanna bikini top between her toes and flung it across the spa. It sailed over the coffee table and landed on one of the leather club chairs. "The cell you're on right now."

"What?" The crinkle of fabric against the receiver crackled in Massie's ears. If she had to guess, it was a raincoat, probably last year's Burberry. "You're breaking up!" Dylan yelled.

Massie selected a tube of indigo Nars and coated each of her lashes twice. "Kristen?"

Kristen swallowed. "Sorry. My mom made me swear not to text till after I finished my homework, and—"

"Am I the only one taking this upgrade seriously?" Massie snapped, layering on another coat of mascara. Her body was starting to feel as heavy as her lashes. How was she supposed to pull off a spa party worthy of high school crushes with no menu, playlist, party games, or conversation topics? "May I remind you that I already have an older crush?"

"I've got a survey," Alicia piped up.

Given. Massie should have known Alicia would come through for her when it came to all things crush-related. She scooted across the floor and leaned against the foot of the leather sofa, allowing herself to relax a little. "Let's hear it."

Alicia cleared her throat, the way she always did before she used her best professional TV journalist voice. "If I were attending a hot spa party hosted by even hotter alphas," she crooned, "I would—"

"Snack on?" Massie prompted eagerly.

"Beluga caviar and a glass of Côte du Rhône."

Huh?

"Listen to?"

"Mozart's Concerto No. 13 in F Major."

The back of Massie's neck was starting to dampen. Were ninth-grade boys notorious for having horrible taste in music? Was she supposed to know that already? Why weren't Dylan and Kristen saying anything?

"Talk about?" she said, hoping her voice wasn't trembling.

"Current trends in international law."

Massie dropped the tube of mascara. "LEESH!" she screeched. "You did nawt survey your dad!"

"He's an older man!" Alicia giggled.

"He's FIFTY!" Massie groaned.

Dylan and Kristen cackled into the receiver.

"You know what?" Massie decided, stomping her bare foot on the carpet. "Never mind. I'll plan it all myself."

"Mass!" Alicia protested. "I was only joking!"

"Exactly," Massie snapped. "And this upgrade is no joking matter. Do you want to be stuck with immature crushes for the rest of your lives?"

Silence.

"I didn't think so. Just bc hcrc Friday at six. And leave Mozart at home." Before her friends could answer, Massie tapped her iPhone screen, ending the call. Then she curled up into a ball at the foot of the sofa, wondering if she could fake bad sushi for the rest of the week.

By Thursday afternoon, the only miracle Claire had witnessed was watching her brother, Todd, finish the rest of his Halloween candy at breakfast without barfing it up on the way to school. So when Layne had texted Claire to meet in the basement bathroom after sixth period to start Phase Two of Operation Save the Males, Claire had agreed. What choice did she have? She was more desperate than the housewives of Orange County, New York, and Atlanta combined.

By the time she found the basement bathroom, which had been roped off and plastered with Layne's handmade sign that read OUT OF ORDER—IT'S PRETTY GROSS IN HERE, Layne was already there, dressed in a long black trench coat, a black fedora, and giant bug-eye sunglasses.

"Thanks for meeting me here, Agent C," she said in a low, serious voice. "Were you followed?" She led Claire across the checkered tile and pushed open the beige door of the handicapped stall, motioning for Claire to go inside.

Claire giggle-rolled her eyes. "This is serious, Layne," she said earnestly, ducking inside the stall and sitting on the closed toilet lid.

"I knooooow." Layne slammed the door shut behind her and slid the metal latch into place. "But do you love this coat, or do you love this coat? I got it at the Salvation Army and it has hooks for all your stuff." Layne undid the frayed sash on her trench and whipped it open. Highlighters, Slim Jims, and Tootsie Pops lined the inside of her coat like she was a fake Rolex vendor on the streets of Manhattan.

"Love it," Claire said hurriedly. "Now can we get started?"

Layne whipped off her sunglasses and pulled her MacBook from her backpack. Then she crouched in the corner, using her bag as a seat cushion, and fired up her computer. "Okay. Got your list?"

Claire reached inside her teal Mossimo triple-handle tote and pulled out her world history notebook. Instead of spending last period taking notes on the decline of the Roman empire, she'd been jotting down ways to convince Massie that upgrading would mean something way worse than Brutus stabbing Caesar: It would mean the complete and total ruin of the Pretty Committee.

OPERATION SAVE THE MALES
PHASE TWO

WHAT'S GREAT ABOUT EIGHTH	WHAT BITES ABOUT NINTH
Eighth-grade alphas = head of the entire school = ULTIMATE ALPHA EXPERIENCE.	Freshmen = bottom of the heap = AUTOMATIC LBRs.
Briarwood crushes! Everybody knows them.	Landon . . . who????
Normal, skin-colored foundation.	Over-bronzing causes cancer. It's true.
Cam Fisher. Cam Fisher's one blue eye. Cam Fisher's one green eye. Cam Fisher's Drakkar Noir cologne. Cam Fisher's ah-dorable smile.	NO CAM FISHER!!!!!!

Those last few selling points were more for Claire than Massie. But hopefully the other points would be enough.

Claire scribbled another heart in the margin next to *green eye*. "Ready?" Layne's idea was to craft fake e-mails about the wonders of eighth, which would "accidentally" be sent to Massie. And it had to work. Because Phase Three was . . . well, Phase Three was nonexistent.

"Just call me Hemingway." Layne's neon green painted fingertips hovered over the glowing keyboard. "Now shoot."

"Ummmmm . . . 'Dear Layne.'" Claire tapped the eraser end of her pencil against her teeth.

"Wrong." Layne shook her head, her fingers still hovering in midair. "You never start your e-mails that way. You always just start with . . . L."

"Okay, fine," Claire sighed, hugging her knees to her chest. "'L.'"

Layne lowered her right index finger to the keyboard. "Done."

"'How are you? I was just thinking about how ah-mazing it is to be in eighth—'"

"Wrong," Layne said again. "Sounds fake."

"Layne! It *is* fake!" Claire huffed, exasperated. She would have taken a deep breath to calm herself down, but the sharp smell of Lysol mixed with the sugary scent of Layne's Hershey's Genuine Chocolate Flavored Bubble Yum lip balm made her want to gag.

Layne lifted her palms in surrender. "Don't shoot the e-mailer," she said, lifting her fedora and scratching the top of her head. "I'm just trying to make sure it sounds natural."

"Right," Claire snorted. "Natural, like your brother's diary?" She air-quoted *your brother's diary,* but instantly regretted it. It wasn't Layne's fault Massie could sniff out a fake entry faster than a Frauda.

Layne snorted. "Fair enough."

Claire rested her chin on her knees. "Okay. 'L. Found some pics of us in seventh the other day. Beyond funny. Can you believe we're almost halfway through eighth?'"

"Better." Layne said, typing Claire's words as she spoke.

"'Being in eighth is waaaaaaaaay cooler than being in seventh.'" Claire consulted her list. "'In eighth, you're the alphas of the whole school.'"

Layne grinned. "Take it slow, Mo."

But Claire was on a roll. "'Plus, crushing on eighth-grade boy alphas is like being alpha squared. So when you're the alphas of the alpha grade, with alpha crushes, it's like the ultimate alpha experience.'"

"Say 'alpha' one more time," Layne deadpanned to her laptop screen.

"It's fine. Massie's fluent in alpha," Claire said. "'That's why I'm so bummed about eventually moving on to ninth,'" she continued, the words automatically rolling off her tongue. "'In ninth, you're at the bottom of the heap again. Which is the opposite of alpha.'"

"Yeaaaah!" Layne's cheer echoed in the deserted bathroom. "Sing it, sister!"

"'I mean, I'm glad Massie has a cute high school crush and all, but to be honest? I'm kinda worried. If she spends all her time with guys in ninth, she'll miss out on the best alpha year of her life! Which would be beyond depressing.'"

"Ayyyy-men!" Layne's fingers flew over the keys.

"And then just sign it 'XO, C,' and send." Claire breathed in Layne's excitement like it was an aromatherapy candle. The letter was Pulitzer worthy. Maybe, just maybe, they'd be able to pull this off after all. And once again, Claire would be responsible for keeping together the Pretty Committee and their crushes.

A nagging thought buzzed at the back of her mind, cutting

through her tingles of triumph. Why was it always up to her to keep her friends from falling apart? If she wasn't saving them from the perils of upgrading, she was reminding them how much they loved one another. She was like a matchmaker for alphas, only without her own show on Bravo.

"Okay, it's sent." Layne nodded. "And now for my reply," she murmured, her face glowing blue in the light of the laptop screen. She opened up a new e-mail and started typing. "'C,'" she read aloud, "'For reals. But I'm sure M knows the deal. Ninth-grade crushes = social death. XO, L.'"

Claire burst out laughing. "Perfect."

"Almost done . . ." The keys clicked beneath Layne's fingers. Suddenly, she stopped and glanced up at Claire with a look of mock horror on her face.

"Ohhhhhhh nooooooo!" With dramatic flair, Layne pressed the back of her hand against her forehead and collapsed against the beige metal wall behind her for support. "I accidentally sent the e-mail to Massie instead of you!" she wailed.

"Ohhhh noooooooooo!" Claire giggle-echoed, lifting her palm to high-five her friend. This plan was a little bit genius and a whole lot foolproof. Massie would read the e-mail, realize what a terrible idea the crush upgrade was, and somehow find a way to convince the Pretty Committee that ninth-grade crushes were more out than Lance Bass.

"Ecc-hem!" A cough sounded in the next stall.

Claire's head snapped toward Layne in disbelief. Layne stared back, her fuchsia-lined eyes wide. But before Claire could say a word, the toilet flushed, and the stall door next to theirs flew open.

"Gig's up, Kuh-laire." Massie's voice sounded on the other side of the door.

"Massie?" Claire slapped her hand against her forehead. Strike two. "What are you doing in the basement bathroom?" Then she turned to Agent L. "Layne!" she hissed. "You didn't check the stalls first?"

Layne pushed herself to her feet, looking sheepish. *Sorry,* she mouthed.

Claire reached for her tote and dragged herself out of the stall.

"Nice try, girls." Massie was standing in front of the sinks, her iPhone in her jeans pocket.

"Huh?" Claire crinkled her nose in a last-ditch attempt, her desperation skyrocketing. "I don't know what you're—"

Yap! Yap! Ya—

"Is that the SnoopDawg Web site?" Claire demanded.

Massie jammed her thumb into her iPhone to silence the barking, but it was too late. Her face went paler than her cream cowl-neck sweater.

The girls stared at one another, their blown cover stories hanging heavy around them in the Lysoled air. After a few beats of silence, Layne snorted. Massie side-glanced at Claire, her glossy lips twitching. Finally, they all cracked up. But even though she was laughing, part of Claire wanted to go back in the stall, lock the door, and cry.

"Ahhhhhh-tention!" Massie twisted the dimmer switch on the tiled wall next to the sauna, plunging the wet section of the spa into complete darkness. She let her fingertips linger on the switch a few seconds longer, the humid darkness shielding her from view while she tried to swallow the 9-karat anxiety lump forming in her throat. "Are you girls ready for your upgrade?"

"Yaaaay!" the PC echoed. When Massie flicked the dial back to position, the track lighting spotlighted Kristen, Dylan, and Alicia, who were perched on the marble edge of the bubbling Jacuzzi, hugging their knees to their chests and bouncing in place like shivering birds on a wire.

"Same," Massie lied, wondering if it was too late to claim bad sushi. Or maybe bad bronzer? Toxic waterproof mascara? Gloss poisoning? She triple-knotted the halter on her canary yellow Milly Shimmer Sorrento bikini top, locking in her A-cups. What had she been thinking, inviting her crush and all his friends to see her in her bathing suit? It was a bigger mistake than Kim Kardashian going blond.

"We need tunes." Kristen leapt off the edge of the tub, her bare feet slapping against the slick tile floor as she headed for the wall-mounted iPod dock next to the shower. "Layne e-mailed me all the songs on her brother's shuffle, and I made a ninth-grade mix." She hovered over the dock, her fluffy center-parted waves falling over her eyes. In seconds, the gravelly sounds of Kings of Leon filled the spa.

"Good thinking." Massie tensed her abs to the rhythm of the churning Jacuzzi jets, hoping to speed-tone them in the last few minutes before Landon arrived.

"Are you gonna take that thing awf?" Dylan wrinkled her nose at Kristen's pink and black Roxy wet suit. "I don't think ninth-grade guys like girls in full-body rubber."

"For one thing," Kristen said defensively, tucking her pouffy hair behind her ears, "this wet suit is exactly like the one Hayden wore to save the dolphins." She gripped the zipper beneath her chin, and with a dramatic flourish, yanked it down to reveal a sporty red two-piece underneath. "Plus, my mom would never let me out of the house in this," she grinned, cranking up the volume on the iPod.

"Ow, ow!" Dylan hooted over a drum solo. "Way hotter."

"Are *you* gonna take *that* thing off?" Alicia dunked the tips of her toes in the Jacuzzi, flicking water at Dylan's gauzy, black floor-length caftan. "'Cause I know ninth-grade guys don't like girls in muumuus." She retied the bows on the sides of her skimpy plaid Burberry bikini.

"But you guys said this was sexy, in a nawt-too-obvious kind of way." Dylan tightened her high pony, looking panicked.

"We meant sexy in a not-obvious-at-all kind of way," Alicia cracked. The humidity in the spa was making her own voluminous waves grow bigger by the second. Was it making her C-cups grow too? Massie could have sworn they weren't this big last week.

"Focus," Massie clapped. She glanced at her reflection in the steamy green glass of the shower stall door. Thanks to one of Jakkob's legendary blowouts, the moisture-dense air couldn't touch her perfectly smooth tresses. Her bright yellow bikini played off the gold flecks in her eyes, and her Pilates-sculpted arms were toned without being Madonna-scary. Objectively, she was a 10, even if her nerves were off the charts.

The spa was a 10 too. In less than a week, Massie, Alicia, Dylan, and Kristen had transformed both themselves and the spa into a high school boy's dream. So her legs ached from canvassing the entire island of Manhattan for the perfect bathing suit. And her index finger and thumb had almost frozen in their AmEx-swiping position. But looking around her, she saw that it had all been worth it.

Fragrant sandalwood drifted through the spa's surround-scent system, replacing the sweet hint of lavender that usually filled the air. The rich, spicy aroma made the spa feel a hundred times more guy friendly. On the flat screen in the dry section, Guitar Hero: Smash Hits was prepped and ready to rock 'n' roll. And in the corner were two fluffy dog beds for Bark and Bean, custom-ordered from Bark Jacobs. Massie had even put together special doggie bags for the puppies, filled with water wings, tiny beach towels, and two miniature lounge chairs for when they wanted to relax Jacuzzi-side.

"So give us the rundown again." Alicia twirled the diamond post in her left ear at top speed.

"Landon's bringing four guys," Massie explained, hovering over the dimmer switch and easing it to the left and right to get the mood lighting perfect. "One for Claire too, in case she comes to her senses in the next few hours."

The girls exchanged glances that said, *Doubt it*.

Massie flicked her hair over her shoulder. "First is Scott. He was the one who DJ'd at the Ho Ho Homeless benefit. Super-tall, blond, blue eyes."

"Mine!" Kristen slapped her rubber-shellacked thigh.

"No fair!" Alicia pouted, elbowing Kristen in the ribs. "I like music."

Kristen elbowed her back. "Well, I like blonds."

"There's more," Massie said reassuringly. "He's also bringing Aidan, who's into photography, Luke, who's some sort of genius on the drums, and Jackson."

"What's he do?" Dylan tugged at her caftan.

Massie shrugged. "I think he's a vegetarian?"

Dylan wrinkled her nose. "Pass."

"Claire can have him," Massie decided. "His eyes are the same color, but apparently one side of his hair is buzzed and the other is ear-length."

"That's kind of the same," Dylan conceded.

Just then, Bark Obama's high-pitched *yap* sounded outside. On cue, Bean sprinted into the spa from the next room, wearing a teeny purple bikini and metallic booties.

"They're here!" the girls whisper-shrieked in their huddle.

"How's my hair?" Alicia hissed, patting her gigantic, humidity-infused waves.

"Fine," Massie said without looking. Even though the spa was warmer than her favorite Theory sweater poncho, goose bumps suddenly surfaced on her oil-slicked skin. "Remember, don't ask them lots of questions about what it's like to be in high school."

"OMG, good call." Kristen fiddled with the zipper of her wetsuit, sliding it up and down.

"And don't say 'OMG' or 'BFF.' In ninth, they think that's immature."

Dylan chewed her bottom lip. "But I don't speak Nine-eeeeese!" she whisper-wailed. "What if I say something stupid?"

"Don't." Massie straightened up and spritzed a final layer of Sephora Super Sheen Bronzing Mist on her face. Then she focused her megawatt smile on the doorway. Her PC upgrade was about to begin. It was more exciting than the opening night of Paris Fashion Week.

"I'm telling you, dude, it was totally off the chain." Landon's friend Scott, in red board shorts and a gray Jimi Hendrix T-shirt, ducked through the doorway first.

"Right?" Landon came in next, carrying Bark, whose paw was cradled in a stylish olive-green nylon sling.

"Oh, heyyyyyy," Massie said casually, like she'd completely forgotten the boys were coming. She took a few cautious steps toward Bark, who shrank into Landon's white cotton V-neck–covered chest.

"What's up?" Landon tossed his dark waves away from his eyes. He lowered Bark to the floor, and the puppy limped excitedly toward Bean, who showered him in tiny tongue kisses.

"Good. I mean, nuh-thing." Massie forced a smile, even though Bark's rejection stung like ocean water on freshly shaved legs. She had sent Bark his own personal invite to her pet-friendly Facebook page and had texted get-well wishes every morning for the past three days. What more could the puppy possibly want?

Three more guys herded through the door behind her crush.

"So this is Aidan, Luke, and Jackson," Landon announced.

"Holla." Aidan lifted his tanned palm, tossing shiny, dark bangs out of his eyes.

Alicia swallowed. "Hey." She batted her thick, quadruple-coated lashes.

"Cool . . . dress?" Luke, a tall blond in brown cargos and a hoodie, nodded at Dylan.

"Uh . . . thanks." Dylan's cheeks flushed redder than Kristen's bikini.

"Kings of Leon!" Scott grin-acknowledged Massie and headed straight for the iPod dock. "This album totally changed my life."

"OMG, me too!" Kristen wiggled out of her wet suit and kick-flicked it across the floor. "I mean . . . yeah. Same."

Jackson, a skinny hipster in gray jeans and a flannel shirt, tucked the jaw-length side of his hair behind his ear. "Thanks for the invite," he said, flashing the girls a smile that almost made up for the half-buzzed cut.

Massie nodded, then refocused on Landon. "So how's Bark?" she asked, crossing her arms over her chest and sucking in her abs. She was glad the Jacuzzi jets were going full-speed. Hopefully, they'd drown out her thumping heart.

"Better." Landon's single dimple looked extra adorable in the dim lighting. "But he could definitely use some Jacuzzi time."

"He's not the only one." Luke tugged his hoodie over his head.

With a deep breath, Dylan gripped her caftan and yanked it off in less than two seconds flat. Then she slid into the Jacuzzi in record time. Alicia and Kristen followed. Massie lingered behind with Landon, who had crouched to the ground and was slipping Bark's sling from around the puppy's shoulder.

"Thanks again for the SnoopDawg," Landon said, straightening up again. His arm brushed against Massie's bronzed skin, sending seismic love waves pulsing through her body. "I've been checking on Bark between classes and stuff. Makes me feel a lot better to keep an eye on him and see what he's up to, ya know?"

"Of course." Massie nodded. "Bean has an extra pair of these, if you want," she said, handing Landon the pair of water wings from Bark's doggie bag.

"Great." Landon scooped Bark off the floor and carried him to the hot tub, sliding on the wings and placing him in the water next to Bean. The puppies closed their eyes, hovering weightlessly in the sandalwood-scented water.

"Man, this place is awesome." Aidan stretched out, semi-putting his arm around Alicia. She blushed and sank lower into the water so the bubbles covered her C-cups.

"Nooooo kidding," Landon groaned, easing in next to Scott.

"You ever see these guys in concert?" Scott asked Kristen, jerking his head toward the iPod, his sandy waves covering one eye. "It's, like, a spiritual experience."

"Seriously?" Kristen looked hypnotized. "Cool."

Massie beamed at her girls, lifting her legs over the edge of the tub. What had she been so nervous about? The upgrade was going smoother than—

"Ehmagawsh!" Claire's voice bounced off the seafoam-colored tiles. "Cam! It's Massie and Landon. And . . . some guys."

Massie whip-turned around, nearly tumbling off the edge of the tub. Claire was standing there with her arms crossed over her gray Old Navy hoodie, arching her white-blond eyebrows smugly. Behind her were Cam, Dempsey, Derrington, and Josh.

Massie felt a tiny bronze sweat droplet slip from the tip of her nose to her left boob, staining her yellow bikini top. And then another. And another. Her confidence, along with her makeup, was disappearing faster than Dylan's Halloween candy stash.

"'Scuze me," Massie wheezed, planting her dripping soles

on the cold marble floor. Whipping a towel around her, she slipped and slid across the spa, leaving faux-tan footprints behind her. Too bad Claire hadn't picked a better outfit. It was definitely gonna be her last.

"We were just in the neighborhood, and we thought we'd stop by." Claire grabbed Cam's arm and dragged him toward the Jacuzzi, smearing Massie's footprints with her Keds along the way. "Hi. I'm Claire," she said, sitting with Cam on the edge of the tub. The rest of the boys filed in behind, leaving Massie seething at the door.

"Hey, girls," Claire sang. "Look who's here!"

Alicia stared down at the bubbles bursting beneath her nose.

Kristen dragged Bean to her chest, pretending to adjust her water wings.

And Dylan's smile evaporated when she saw Derrington, whose soccer uniform was on backward.

"Hey." Luke, Aidan, Scott, and Jackson nodded at the guys.

But the PC's ex-crushes just stood there. Massie debated making a break for the main house and leaving the girls to fend for themselves. But she'd never make it barefoot all the way to the house without destroying her pedi. Plus, giving up would mean Claire had won. So she stalked back to the Jacuzzi in her makeup-stained suit. Why hadn't she thought to bring a backup?

"You get dressed in the mirror or something?" Luke cracked, craning his neck toward Derrington.

Aidan snorted and clapped Luke on the shoulder.

Dylan sank a little lower in the hot tub. The water level was inching past her lips and tickling her nose. She looked like she wanted to sink to the bottom and disappear forever.

"Lost a bet." Derrington finally spoke up, without tearing his gaze away from Dylan. He shrugged. "What're you gonna do?"

"I hear ya," Luke nodded sympathetically. "One time I lost a bet and had to shave my whole body."

"Ew!" Alicia squealed, then slapped her palm over her mouth.

"For real?" Derrington's eyes lit up. "Like"—he lowered his voice—"everything?"

Luke nodded solemnly.

"Awwwwesome!" Derrington bellowed. He lumbered over to the hot tub, wearing his soccer cleats on the wrong feet. Massie sucked in a sharp breath, resisting the urge to trip him. Even though he deserved it for showing up uninvited.

"You guys go to Briarwood?" Aidan asked.

"Yeah," Cam nodded.

"I heard the new building was really sweet," Jackson said, leaning back as Bean and Bark doggie-paddled laps across the Jacuzzi.

"Is this the new Kings of Leon?" Dempsey examined the iPod dock on the wall. "Track eight is, like . . . spiritual." He turned up the volume and rocked out on air drums. The vibrations from the bass made Massie's entire body shake. Or maybe that was pure rage.

"No way!" Scott jumped up, soaking Kristen's hair. Her

pouffy waves shriveled instantly. "I was just saying that." He glanced down at Kristen. "Wasn't I just saying that?"

Eh-ma-OUT! Massie wanted to scream. Then she wanted to strangle Claire with the laces from Derrington's cleats. She probably would have, if she wasn't so sure Landon would think that was a quote-unquote "immature" way to handle conflict.

Dylan's, Kristen's, and Alicia's eyes all widened in panic, silently begging Massie to do something. But she was too shocked to think straight. Their exes weren't supposed to be friends with their upgrades! It was unnatural! The only people in the history of the universe to make it work were Demi, Ashton, and Bruce. And nobody believed them anyway.

"Guitar Hero! Smash Hits!" Josh yelled from the dry section.

"Score!" Derrington hobbled-ran toward the glass door that separated the wet and dry sections of the spa. Dempsey followed, like Josh had just announced he was giving away free hundred-dollar bills with a side of cheese fries.

Finally. When the last of the exes had crossed over into the next room, Massie slid the glass door shut and turned the lock with a satisfying click, separating the men from the boys.

"Claire? Cam?" Massie sang, crossing back toward the tub. "Jacuzzi?" She lifted a fluffy towel from the top of the stack and whipped it at Claire with extra force.

Claire ducked, and the towel sailed over her head. "No thanks. Forgot my suit," she mumbled.

"Too bad." Massie sat on the cool marble edge of the

Jacuzzi and slid into the steamy water next to Landon. "Sorry about that," she said as she giggle-shifted a little closer to him, breathing in the scent of his CK Eternity Summer cologne and allowing herself to relax for the first time all night. Dempsey and Derrington could eat their hearts out. Not that they were paying any attention. But still. "You know middle-school boys. Sooo immature." She exchanged knowing glances with the rest of the PC.

Bean poked out her tongue in agreement, lapping up the scented Jacuzzi water. Then she scooted across the hot tub toward Landon and Massie. Bark nipped her tiny purple bikini bottoms between his teeth, dragging behind.

"No worries," Landon assured her.

Pulling Bean toward her, Massie glanced up at Claire and Cam. Skin flushed and arms crossed tightly over her chest, Claire was obviously furious. But from her spot on Cloud Nine, Massie was finding it hard to care.

CURRENT STATE OF THE UNION

IN	OUT
ADD	BOCD
Hot-tubbing with Niners	Hobnobbing with Eighters
Upgrading	Same-grading

"And then she goes, 'Kuh-laire? Is this the OCD Spring Fling?'" Claire huffed, pacing back and forth between the rumpled chocolate-colored duvet on her bed and the window that looked over the Blocks' main house. "'Cause we don't need chaperones.'"

"Ha!" Layne's snort blared from the Dell laptop on Claire's white wooden desk. The computer teetered precariously atop a pile of desk clutter, which included a few back issues of *CosmoGirl,* a flyer with the Briarwood Tomahawks' home game schedule highlighted in pink, and an open French workbook.

Claire resumed her Skype-rant. "So I told her I wasn't gonna chaperone her sleepover, either, and we left." Claire whipped back the aqua piqued-silk panel that hung over her window. Massie's windows were dark, which meant the PC was sleeping in the spa tonight. Good. The last thing Claire wanted was to watch her friends giggling about their new crushes. "Can you believe her?"

"Actually, yeah." A sharp, crunching sound filled the room. It felt like sandpaper rubbing against Claire's last nerve. She stalked over to the speakers and turned down the volume. "We're talking about Massie Block, remember?"

"I know." Claire shoved up the sleeves of her Powerpuff Girls pajamas and yanked out her wooden desk chair. She hadn't worn these since she'd moved to Westchester, and she was way too old for them now. But there was something comforting about the soft, worn fabric. It reminded her of a simpler time.

"The Massie Block who threw salmon at you and dumped gazpacho on your head when you first moved here?" Layne was sitting cross-legged on her own bed, a giant bowl of pretzels mixed with Halloween candy in her lap. Her handmade bejeweled SAVE THE MALES: DON'T BE A H8R tee glinted in the light of the undulating lava lamp nearby. "The Massie Block who tricked you out of wearing the Dirty Devil Halloween costume she wore last year? The Massie—"

"I get it, Layne." Claire plopped into the chair, sitting on a crumpled pair of Massie hand-me-down AG Jeans. The button dug into the back of her thigh. She yanked the pants out from under her and flung them across the room. They landed in a defeated heap on the carpet. "But that was last year. We weren't friends yet."

Layne shrugged, digging a handful of pretzel mix from the green plastic bowl in her lap. "Just saying," she mumbled over a mouthful, "I don't get why you seem so surprised whenever Massie does something mean."

"Claaaaaaaaaiiiiiirrrrree!" Judi Lyons's voice sounded from the kitchen, over the labored churn of the dishwasher. "You in for family game night?"

"In a minute, Mom!" Claire yelled back.

"Easy!" Layne slapped her palms over her ears.

"Sorry," Claire said. Absentmindedly, she pulled a red colored pencil from her drawer and doodled a tiny heart on the chipped white desktop, bearing down harder than usual. The desk was covered with different-colored sketches, symbols, and notes, more than half of them Cam-related. "It's not just Massie," she said. "It's everybody else. I mean, how can they be so shallow? How can they not even care that they're ditching their crushes for these new guys they don't even know?" She re-outlined an old CL ♥ CF note from seventh.

Layne swallowed. "So how'd Dempsey look?" She smoothed her unruly brown waves and licked the pretzel crumbs from her hot pink glossed lips.

Claire ignored her, staring at the giant corkboard that hung over her desk. It was covered in photos of Claire and Massie, blowing kisses in the back of the Range Rover . . . Claire and Dylan, clinking plastic spoons at Pinkberry . . . Claire, Kristen, and Alicia in their trampire costumes, making sexy-scary pouts in Massie's entrance hall. The girl in those pictures looked like Claire. And she even looked happy. Like she fit in with the perfectly glossy girls in the photographs. "It's like their souls got sucked on Halloween, and now they've changed into these girls who don't care about anybody but themselves."

Layne snorted, spraying a shower of chocolatey pretzel bits into the webcam lens. She licked her finger and wiped the bits away, leaving Claire with a partially brown-smudged view. "Claire. These girls have never cared about anybody but themselves. They've always been this shallow." She paused, her brow crinkling like she was constipated. "Maybe they're not the ones who've changed. Maybe you're the one who's gotten your soul sucked."

The harsh reality of Layne's words felt like a knockout punch to the gut. But maybe the words hurt so much because they were true. She'd traded her old Levi 501s for Sevens and her short, fluffy bangs for brow-skimming, razor-cut ones. Her outsides definitely looked different . . . did her insides look different now too?

"Maybe you're right." Suddenly, Claire's limbs felt heavy, like they were filled with lead. "Maybe I have changed." She closed her burning eyes, flashing back to the very first moment her Keds had crossed over the threshold to Massie Block's world. Standing in the middle of Massie's spotless white iPad in denim overalls and homemade jewelry, Claire had felt like a cheap pleather bag that had accidentally been thrown in with a display of calfskin totes when no one was looking. She was like Splenda to Massie's sugar, or flip-flips to her Ferragamos.

What would her life be like now if the Lyons hadn't moved into the Blocks' guesthouse when they'd gotten to Westchester? What would she be like? Would she still be wearing friendship bracelets instead of hand-me-down gold bangles? Would she have friends like her old friends in Orlando, who didn't care about labels or older boys?

Wiping her mental slate clean, she tried to picture a life

without the constant stress of Pretty Committee breakups and makeups. Without the pressure of having her outfit rated every day at school, or always feeling like she was trying to catch up with Massie and Alicia. But her mind was totally blank. The Pretty Committee had become her life.

But what if she didn't want it to be?

"Maybe you guys are growing apart." Layne lifted the snack bowl to her lips and shook the dusty pretzel remains into her mouth before sending it sailing across the room like a giant Frisbee. Leftover pretzel salt clung to her lips like fairy dust. "No big deal. Happens all the time." She fell back onto a pile of puff-painted pillows, leaving Claire with a view of only her neck, chin, and nose.

"Really?" Claire said dejectedly, trying not to stare up Layne's cavernous nostrils.

"Yeah." Layne's neck jostled as she talked, reminding Claire of the way Judi Lyons's arm fat jiggled when she waved. "That's what happened with me and Heather and Meena. Why d'you think I've been hanging out with you guys so much lately?"

"CLAAAAAAAAIIIIIRRRE!" Judi called again. "You want the thimble or the top hat?"

"TOP HAT!" Claire screeched.

"No way! That's mine!" Todd yelled from the living room.

"FINE!" Claire rolled her eyes. "THIMBLE!" When she glanced back at her screen, Layne was holding two pillows on either side of her head like fluffy white Princess Leia buns. "Oops. Sorry."

"Claire." Layne released her downy earmuffs. "Seriously."

"I think . . ." Claire chewed at the inside of her cheek, staring down at her desk. "I think I'm ready to find some new friends." The second the words left her mouth, her eyes fell on a bright purple glitter scribble Massie had added to Claire's desk graffiti at the end of the summer. Underneath a rough sketch of a charm bracelet, Massie had written PC4L. And next to it, a purple paw print, for Bean.

Suddenly, Claire whip-turned toward her window, as if Massie could be eavesdropping all the way from the spa. Her pulse quickened. Would looking for new friends make her just as bad, just as finicky as the rest of the PC? She shook the thought from her head. This wasn't the same. It wasn't like she wanted to ditch her old friends. She just wanted to find a few new ones to hang out with too. Friends who liked Halloween candy and eighth-grade boys.

"Are you for real?" Suddenly, Layne sounded exhausted. "'Cause I don't think I can take another PC breakup. You guys've worn me down."

"It won't be like a breakup," Claire dug her thumb into her desktop, chipping away at the purple charm bracelet. "I'm not totally leaving the PC. Swear."

"I don't knooooow." Layne wrinkled her nose. "Massie's not gonna liiiiiike it."

"She's so into Landon and these new guys, she won't even notice when I'm not there." Claire crossed her fingers and sat on them until they went numb. Maybe she hadn't completely thought this through.

"Where are you supposed to get new friends anyway?" Layne plugged in a crimping iron next to her bed and started transforming her parched waves into frizzy kinks.

"Uhhhh, I . . . dunno." Okay, she definitely hadn't thought this through. Did Skype have a REWIND button? Wait. No. Claire screwed her eyes shut, squeezing the doubt from her brain. So what if Massie didn't like Claire having other friends. Wasn't it a free country? Didn't she deserve to be happy? "Where do you even meet new friends?"

"Um . . ." Layne tilted her head to one side.

"CLAAAAAIIIRRRE!" Judi, Jay, and Todd synchroscreamed from the living room. "Your turn!"

Claire shoved back her chair and stalked over to her door, throwing it open.

"Count me out!" she yelled. "I'm busy!" Then she slammed the door again and resumed her position.

Layne was upright again and scribbling furiously on a Hello Kitty notepad. "Got some ideas," she murmured, dropping the left, crimped side of her head toward her shoulder. "Hold on . . ."

Claire swallowed the faint taste of pennies that had deposited itself in the back of her throat. Her eyes traveled over the photo board again, over the memories that she had created with the Pretty Committee. Only this time, the pictures seemed faded. Stiff. Maybe it was time for some new memories. Maybe Claire was ready to see the world through a whole new lens.

"Okay." She leaned toward her laptop screen, looking Layne dead in the eye. "I'm ready." It was time for an upgrade of her own.

Wrapped in a fluffy white spa robe, Massie was trying hard to concentrate on the open algebra text propped against her knees. But not even the steaming mug of ginkgo biloba–infused pomegranate tea on her nightstand could help her focus on slope-intercept equations. Not when the sweet smell of Landon Crane's cologne still lingered on her robe. Burying her nose in her shoulder, she took a long, deep breath. The soft cotton fibers smelled like true love. The rare kind that existed between Ellen and Portia. Penn and Blake. Kanye and himself.

And now, Landon and Massie.

Bean, who was napping on an overstuffed sham at the foot of the bed, let out a satisfied sigh, her tiny pink tongue hanging happily from the corner of her mouth. Massie wondered if Bean was dreaming about her crush too.

Focus. She turned her attention back to her workbook and read the first problem: *Find the equation of the straight line that has slope m = 4 and passes through the point (-1, -6).*

Out of the corner of her eye, Massie's sleeping MacBook was blinking. Inviting her to check the SnoopDawg Web site for a quick Landon fix. A white, glowing beacon, the slowly pulsing battery light seemed to call out to her:

Lan-don. Lan-don. Lan-don.

At her feet, Bean's rhythmic sighs seemed to whisper:
Cuh-rane. Cuh-rane. Cuh-rane.

And on the bedside table next to her, the second hand on her white, round-faced alarm clock ticked:

Snoop. Dawg. Snoop. Dawg. Snoop. Dawg.

It was official: The universe was dying for her to catch a glimpse of her crush. Probably because the universe understood the agony that came with a Landon-free weekend. It seemed like years since the spa party, since she'd watched his dimple deepen every time he laughed at her jokes. And even though he'd sent an adorable thank-you text quote-unquote "from Bark" on Saturday morning, going forty-eight hours without actually seeing him just didn't feel right. It was like eating sushi without wasabi. Watching television without TiVo. Wearing Dolce without Gabbana.

Ugh! It was time for a distraction. She flipped her math notebook to a blank page and grabbed her favorite glittery purple gel pen.

TOP 10 REASONS I ♥ LANDON CRANE

10. The way his one dimple deepens when he laughs at all my comebacks. Bonus points for sense of humor.

9. He's in ninth, which means he's nine times more mature than ex-crushes Derrington and Dempsey.

8. His ah-mazing blue-green eyes, which change colors depending on what I'm wearing, so we'll never clash.

7. He never wears shorts in the winter like Derrington. Or wiggles his butt when he's happy. Or ditches me just because he has to quote-unquote "go to soccer practice" or he'll quote-unquote "get kicked off the team." Puh-lease.

6. He's not into theater like Dempsey. Or Africa. Or volunteering.

5. Bark Jacobs, his mom's posh pet spa—slash—boutique. Automatic wardrobe upgrade for Bean!!!

4. Bark Obama, his ah-dorable pug. Automatic crush for Bean!!!

3. His wardrobe is almost as good as mine. Plus, he looked amazing on the runway at my Ho Ho Homeless benefit, without stealing the focus. He's ahbviously confident enough to let his crush shine.

2. The way his name sounds when I say it out loud: *Landon Crane. Landon Crane. Landon Crane.*

1. HE'S IN NINTH! Having an older crush = ALPHA & BEYOND.

Massie put down the pen and sighed. All those facts were true, but they didn't tell her what Landon was doing *right now.* And the sleep light on her Mac was blinking almost hypnotically now.

Lan-don. Lan-don. Lan-don.

Finally, she couldn't take the torture anymore. She reached for her laptop, flipped it open, and typed the SnoopDawg URL into the Web browser. Immediately, a puppy in a Sherlock Holmes outfit with a magnifying glass in its paw sniffed its way across the screen, signaling that the site was loading. The anticipation made her stomach churn like Jacuzzi jets on full blast, and she felt giddier than Claire did before a study date with Cam.

Thoughts of her crush were suddenly replaced with thoughts of Claire, who had ditched the sleepover to do Gawd knew what else. She'd claimed bad gummies, but that was obviously code for *I've got something better to do*. Only, what plans could Claire possibly have that didn't involve the Pretty Committee? Not knowing exactly what Claire was up to made Massie feel more uneasy than the time at the mall she'd gotten distracted on her cell and accidentally wandered into the Dress Barn instead of BCBG. It was strange and unfamiliar territory, and no self-respecting alpha belonged there.

When the site loaded, a herd of cartoon puppies flounced into view, *yap*-prompting Massie to enter Bark's ID number in the doghouse graphic in the middle of the screen. Bean's eyelids fluttered open, and she scampered across the duvet, collapsing in an excited heap in the crook of Massie's arm.

"It's not that Claire doesn't want to hang out with us anymore, Bean." With her right hand, Massie typed in the ID number and password that had come with the charm, while she scratched behind Bean's ears with her left. If she'd had an extra set of fingers, she would have crossed them that Landon hadn't changed Bark's password yet. "It's just that she's obviously not ready to upgrade. She's kind of young for thirteen."

Bean wrinkled her pug nose, obviously sympathetic.

"I know. It's beyond frustrating," Massie nodded, feeling slightly better that she wasn't the only one to notice Claire's immaturity. "But if we're really her friends, we can't control what she does. We just have to give her time to mature and realize that . . ."

She clicked ENTER and screwed her eyes shut. Slowly, she opened her left eye a crack.

The cartoon puppies trotted into the doghouse, and the screen went black. Then a grainy, dim image of a puppy paw invaded the screen.

She was in.

"Yesssss!" Massie leaned forward, squinting at the screen like Kendra squinted at *Vogue* when she misplaced her reading glasses. Fuzzy claws scraped and scratched at the camera lens, completely obstructing Massie's view of anything Landon-related.

"Baaaaark," Massie moaned. "Quit messing with your collar!"

Bean lapped at the screen, leaving behind a trail of drool.

"Ewwwww," Massie giggle-chided her puppy as she swiped the drool away with the sleeve of her robe.

Seconds later, the camera dropped to the floor, leaving Massie with the same view of Landon's room she'd have if she were in downward-facing dog position in yoga class. She leaned closer, the tip of her nose almost smudging the screen. Unexpectedly, she was drenched with a fresh wave of adoration for her crush. Landon's room confirmed what she already knew: that he was meant for her. The John Mayer Trio poster over his bed proved he was poetic. The olive-green duvet and 600 thread-count (give or take) sheets said he was stylish enough to care about home decor, but the chocolate brown throw pillows strewn haphazardly across the bed said he didn't care too much. And the Prada sneakers peeking out from under his bed screamed *style, style, style*.

Then the screen went black.

"Ehmagawd!" Massie gripped the sides of her laptop screen and shook it like an Etch A Sketch. A drool-slicked pink tongue and a mouthful of tartar-stained teeth appeared as the camera twisted and turned, making Massie feel queasy.

"Bark!" she screeched at the screen. Bean shot to the foot of the bed, chasing her tiny tail in frantic circles. "Do NAWT eat the SnoopDawg! Bad puppy! Bad!"

As if he could hear her desperation, Bark spat out the camera, and the drool-soaked lens bounced and rolled into the middle of Landon's room. Massie fell back onto her pillows, exhausted. A chilly breeze from her cracked bedroom window wafted past her lavender curtains and over her bed.

She burrowed deeper beneath her duvet, keeping her eyes on the screen.

A pair of Puma Black Labels and dark-wash denim–covered ankles crossed in front of the camera. Massie shot upright again.

"Landon!" she squealed, her heart revving beneath her ribs as the camera teased her with a tiny taste of her crush. From the expertly faded wash around the hem of his jeans, Massie could tell Landon was wearing Paper Denim & Cloth. It was the perfect choice for a crisp fall Sunday.

Then a second pair of ankles filled the screen next to Landon's. Only these ankles weren't boy ankles. They were bronzed, freshly shaved, and slender.

Massie swallowed hard. These were girl ankles. Maybe even alpha-girl ankles.

She reached for the oversize mug on her bedside table and took a gulp. The steaming tea scorched her tongue. But she barely even noticed the pain over the tidal wave of jealousy surging inside her.

Above the ankles, a pair of bleach-stained jeans were rolled up to mid-calf. Below the cuffs were low, gray suede booties. It was a riskier fashion choice than Fergie's harem pants. But somehow, like the harem pants, it worked.

Leaning closer, Massie could make out the outline of a tiny pink hummingbird floating above a daisy, just above the ankle bone. Her jaw dropped. A tattoo? Did that make the mystery girl tacky, trashy, or edgy? Massie had no idea how to tell.

The gray booties stepped back from the camera. Bean

growled as Bark leapt into Ankle-Bird's arms. She was wearing a fitted boyfriend blazer over a white ribbed tank, with a tangle of long necklaces swinging from her neck. Her hands were freshly manicured, and she wore a sparkly vintage cocktail ring on her left middle finger.

"Show. Me. Your. Face!" Massie demanded, tiny beads of sweat forming along her temple. How could she tell whether the girl was a threat if she couldn't rate her hair?

Bean bared her teeth at the screen as Bark licked Ankle-Bird's hand happily. Massie wanted to soothe her puppy, but how could she when she needed soothing herself? She closed her eyes, desperate to regain control.

"You are strong. You are confident," she said, repeating her confidence mantra. "And no one can take your strength away from you. . . ."

Opening her eyes, she snuck another peek. Watching Landon with another girl was like watching *The Biggest Loser:* It hurt, but she just couldn't help herself.

Next to Landon, Ankle-Bird produced an envelope from the green Diesel messenger bag slung across her torso. Then she handed it to him.

Was it a bill? A note? A love letter?

Landon tore it open, obviously curious. At the top of the page, an ink paw print was followed by a date and time that were too blurry to make out.

An invitation to a high school party.

Massie took a slow, deep breath that turned into a heaving, rasping choke.

Because instead of handing Ankle-Bird a note that said, I ♥ MASSIE BLOCK AND WOULD SOONER WEAR GENERIC-BRAND DENIM THAN ATTEND A PARTY WITHOUT HER, Landon folded it carefully and slipped it into his back pocket.

He may as well have stabbed Massie in the heart with Ankle-Bird's gray suede heel.

Ankle-Bird lifted Bark from the floor and stood up. Landon followed, and soon, all Massie could see was his empty room. Suddenly, the John Mayer poster seemed cliché, the Pradas outdated. Massie hadn't noticed before, but those were definitely two seasons old. At least.

Swiping her emergency sample vial of Chanel No. 19 from under her pillow, Massie speed-spritzed it and sucked in the flowery scent of jasmine and ylang-ylang, like the vial was an inhaler and she was a band geek in the throes of a debilitating asthma attack. The familiar scent slowed her breathing slightly.

Who was she kidding? Landon was still perfect for her, John Mayer and outdated Pradas aside.

Screwing her eyes shut, Massie tried her confidence mantra again.

"You are strong. You are confident. And no one can take your strength away from you."

She wanted to believe it was true. But the words felt more fake than those ninth-grade girls' spray tans on Halloween night. She slapped her laptop screen shut and curled up in a terry cloth–covered ball, waiting for the tears to come. But instead of sadness, all she felt was anger.

There was no way she was going to have another crush stolen from her. Not again. Landon Crane was the most alpha ninth-grade crush a girl could ask for, and Massie was his plus-one. Together, they scored a perfect ten. If Massie had to fight to keep Ankle-Bird out of the equation, she'd fight. But first, she had to find the tattooed crush-stealer.

Those gray suede booties could run, but they couldn't hide.

Claire had made the trip from her locker to the New Green Café so many times before, she could have done it blindfolded. But today, everything about her usual route felt different. The cast of musical theater kids belting the entire score of *Wicked* outside the auditorium seemed free-spirited instead of off-key. The PETA Club papering the lockers with enough I'D RATHER GO NAKED flyers to wipe out the rain forest seemed progressive instead of self-righteous. Even the girl in seventh who spent every lunch period reading *The Lord of the Rings* on a picnic blanket next to her locker seemed like a mysterious, brooding intellectual instead of just a speed bump along the way to the café.

It was as if Claire had gone through her entire life at OCD with blinders on, and now she was seeing everyone her school had to offer with Lasik-sharpened vision. How could she have been so worried about finding new friends? The social options at OCD were endless. All she had to do was choose.

The traffic in the halls was rush-hour slow, and it took Claire a full three minutes to cover the ground between her locker and the girl's bathroom. Eyes on the café's frosted glass doors, she elbowed her way through an obstacle course of messenger bags and bleating cell phones, getting more impatient by the second.

Ducking past a Burberry plaid–covered shoulder, she sighed at the insistent beeping that seemed to follow her all the way to the café. This was exactly what was wrong with Westchester. Back in Orlando, only a few of her friends had cell phones. But here, phones were a necessity, as indispensable as underwear. It was so annoy—

"Hey." A girl from Claire's last-period class arched her eyebrow at the patchwork leather bag slung over Claire's shoulder. "Your cell is giving me a migraine."

"Oh. Thanks." *Whoops.* Claire unearthed her cell from the bottom of her bag.

Layne: Where u b, C? Surprise waiting 4 u in the café. Meet inside the doors ASAP.
Layne: P.S. Like ur new ringtone? I programmed while u weren't looking. ;)

Claire shoved her phone back in her bag, hurrying toward the café as fast as her Uggs, and the student-clogged hallway, would allow. As usual, Layne was being super-secretive about her plans. But that made Claire's friend upgrade seem more exciting than a parent-free study date with Cam.

When Claire finally made it into the café, Layne was waiting by the Smartwater dispenser inside the doors, balancing a rainbow glitter–covered velvet ring box on her nose like a trained seal.

"Hey! Ten seconds," she bragged, wobbling back and forth with zero regard for the line forming behind her for the vending machine. The brass medals clinging to the shoulder of her six-sizes-too-big camo jacket jangled as she moved. "Eleven. Twel—"

"My surprise?" Claire swiped the box and popped it open. Inside was a silver-plated ring featuring a large black center stone.

"My best invention yet," Layne said proudly, yanking the ring from its velvet nest. "I call it the BFFinder. You put it on, and the stone turns red when you're getting close to somebody cool. It turns black when you're around people you're not compatible with. Patent pending."

"Huh," Claire sniffed, accidentally inhaling some of the glitter on the box. When she sneezed, a few specks of silver glitter shot from her nostrils and fell to the floor. It felt like a sign. From this moment on, Claire Lyons was totally free of all things glitz and glamour—free of all the superficial trappings she'd acquired since her arrival in Westchester. She was getting a fresh new start. And there was nothing wrong with that . . . right? She resisted the urge to sneak a peek at Table 18.

"Allow me to demonstrate." Layne jammed the ring on her finger and dragged Claire through the bamboo table labyrinth, stopping at a random table of all-black–wearing sixth-graders. Layne thwacked the nearest one with the ring.

"Ow!" The girl rubbed her shoulder through her World of Warcraft tee.

"See?" Layne lifted her finger. The stone was still black.

"Not compatible." She clapped the sixth-grader on the back and bounded for her regular lunch table.

Sorry, Claire mouthed before stepping over a dried blob of soy cheese on the floor to follow her friend. The striped tie Layne had looped around her jeans as a makeshift belt fluttered behind her like the streamers on Claire's old bike. Thinking of her bike made her think of Cam, which made her think of the spa party the week before, which made her want to check on Massie all over again. Was she angry at Claire for switching lunch tables? Or worse, hurt? Claire's stomach seized at the thought.

"Wanna try it?" Layne careened into the side of Table 23 and sat. Three neatly folded copies of the *New York Times* had been placed at the head of the table. "See if it fits." Layne wrenched the ring over her knuckle with a groan.

"Thanks." Claire's gaze swooped over to Table 18, like there was a magnetic force between her and the PC that was impossible to fight. The girls were leaning together in an airtight huddle over untouched plates of vegan mac 'n' cheese and seitan skewers with peanut sauce. Were they gossiping about their new crushes? Worse, were they gossiping about her, thinking she'd ditched them?

Claire had the sudden urge to compose a quick text-planation so the PC would understand. Although maybe they wouldn't care as much as she'd thought they would. When she'd broken the news to Massie that she was having lunch with Layne to meet a few new friends, Massie hadn't batted a lash. She hadn't threatened Claire with PC dismissal or revoked Range Rover privileges for the week. In fact, she'd kind of seemed to understand. Claire's ruby angora hoodie was starting to feel itchy all over. If all she was doing was broadening her horizons a little, why was she starting to feel like more of a player than Beckham?

The PC's huddle loosened, and Massie caught Claire's eye from the head of the table. Claire lifted her hand in a wave. Massie blinked coolly but half smiled back. She was obviously trying hard to be flexible. Less controlling. And Claire knew her well enough to know that being less Lycra required more effort than her annual pre-bikini season carb fast. Had Massie really changed since the PC's big fight? Was Claire the one being unfair, by not giving Massie a chance to show her true colors?

"Claire." Layne flicked the ring in Claire's direction, and it skittered across the table. "You gonna try it on, or what?"

Not wanting to hurt Layne's feelings, Claire slid the ring over her middle finger. The stone instantly turned puke green.

"So we're having lunch with Bill Gates," Layne announced. "I tried to get Oprah and Shakespeare, but they couldn't make it on such short notice."

"Huh?" The ring felt weighty on Claire's finger. She dropped her hand casually to her lap, secretly tilting it toward the Pretty Committee's table. Was she close enough to get a read? According to the BFFinder, were she and the PC compatible? She forced herself to look. But the stone was still puke-colored. Not realizing she'd been holding her breath, she exhaled.

"You know," Layne was saying impatiently, "from the Witty Committee. Just to see if you guys get along."

"Oh. Right." Layne and Kristen's Witty Committee was a group of super-smart OCD'ers who got together to . . . actually, Claire had no idea what the Witty Committee did.

"But this is just to road test the ring," Layne qualified, snapping open her copy of the *Times*. "You can't actually join the Witty Committee unless you're, like, a genius." She smiled into the World News section.

Before Claire had the chance to bristle, Bill Gates appeared across from her.

"Greetings."

Danh Bondok was a tech genius–slash–exchange student Massie had christened "Candy Corn" because of his yellow teeth. He was smiling and holding a sweating brown bag that smelled like coconut curry.

Claire forced a smile. "Hey, Cand—" She caught herself just in time. "I mean, Danh."

"Call me Bill." Danh-slash-Bill-slash–Candy Corn deposited his lunch on the table and hitched up his already ankle-skimming Dockers, revealing hairy, pencil-thin ankles. He sat down across from Claire and grinned nervously.

"'Kay . . . Bill," Claire said uncertainly.

"Check the ring," Layne hissed excitedly.

Claire checked. "What's green mean again?"

Layne shrugged. "I'm still working out the kinks."

"Claire," Bill Gates said politely, poking the bridge of his glasses until they skidded up his nose, "Layne tells me you're into photography." He tore open his brown bag and pulled out a plastic container of noodles, popping the top and digging in.

"Um, yeah." Claire nodded, temporarily ravaged by the spicy-sweet scent of curry.

"I'm a bit of an Ansel Adams buff myself," Danh said. "His use of sharp focus and heightened contrast is pretty genius, don't you think?"

Layne nodded, like Danh had been speaking English the whole time. "Totally."

"Uhhhhhh." Claire scratched the back of her neck, which was damp with sweat. "Sure."

Danh shot Layne a look. Was that pity? Or curry-induced indigestion?

"So Bill," Layne said, obviously trying to change the subject, "tell us what's new with you."

Dahn nodded. "Well, as we're all aware, the Vista operating system has been found to have several irreparable design flaws." His dark eyes settled on Claire, waiting for her to contribute.

"Yeah. It's really . . . too bad." Claire dug her nail into her thigh, hating how the words sounded coming out of her mouth. Why couldn't they talk about something she actually had an opinion on, like the Maksim-Karina breakup or Serendipity's new line of gourmet-flavored gummies?

Dahn's thick black eyebrows slanted in disappointment.

"Anyway, it looks like Microsoft is going to have to say, 'Hasta la . . . VISTA' to the old version." He paused, fighting a smile.

While Danh and Layne cracked up, Claire checked the ring again. Still puke green. Maybe the ring was better at detecting her mood than she'd thought.

By last period, the familiarity of the Pretty Committee was starting to feel as enticing as Cam's extra-large Briarwood fleece. Maybe the fit wasn't perfect, but at least it was comfortable.

Luckily, Layne wasn't in Claire's last-period study hall, which gave Claire a fighting chance of getting out to the parking lot undetected. So when Mr. Myner shoo-dismissed the class five minutes early, Claire jerked her backpack out of her locker and made a break for it, trying to ignore the guilt itch creeping down her neck. Sure, Layne was only trying to help, but how was wrist-dragging Claire down the hall, shoving the BFFinder in everyone's face, actually helping? So far, Claire had zero new friends and one rapidly developing case of carpal tunnel.

There had to be an easier way.

Golden afternoon sunlight poured through the open double doors at the end of the main building hallway, promising freedom, a giant bowl of Cinammon Toast Crunch, and an afternoon bike ride with Cam. Just a few . . . more . . . steps . . .

Three feet from the doors, two hands clamped over her eyes.

"Ahhhhhhh!" Claire yelled, feeling a knot tighten at the

back of her head. Her hands flew to her face, clawing at the synthetic blindfold now squeezing her throbbing brain.

"Surpriiiiise!" Layne's hot breath smelled like guacamole-flavored sours, her new favorite afternoon snack.

So close . . . Now Claire knew how Bean must have felt after a full day of trying on themed Halloween costumes for Massie: exhausted, defeated, and too weak to fight back.

"What's next?" Claire asked warily, ignoring a round of giggles that was obviously directed at her.

Layne gripped Claire by the arms and swung her around in a full 180-degree turn. "One more stop for the day. You're gonna love this one. Pinky-swear." She shoved Claire forward.

Claire's left shoulder collided into someone, knocking her counterclockwise.

"Careful, you two," a gruff man's voice warned. "No horseplay in the halls." Claire tensed, the scent of chalk dust and stale coffee overpowering her heightened sense of smell.

"Sorry, Mr. Myner. Sir." Claire backed into Layne, almost tripping over her squeaking rain boots.

"Oops!" Layne whisper-giggled. "Myner oversight on my part."

"Ha ha," Claire snapped, rubbing her throbbing shoulder. Just to be safe, she extended her hands in front of her as a buffer.

"Almost there." Layne guided Claire awkwardly through the halls like they were a pair of amateur figure skaters hitting the ice for the first time together. The slam of locker doors, clicking of padlocks, and rustle of ballet flats swirled around her in the wavy darkness.

Finally, Layne yanked back on the blindfold knot, jerking Claire to a halt.

Claire ripped off her sweaty blindfold, rubbing guacamole-scented tears out of her eyes. They were standing outside the OCD art studio.

"You weren't supposed to take off the blindfold till I said," Layne pouted, loosening the knot on her striped tie belt and securing it back around her hips. She gripped the smudged silver door handle and hip-bumped the door open. "Come on."

Claire followed cautiously behind, finger-fluffing the blindfold crease in her hair.

"Ta-daaaaaaaa." Layne stepped aside, spreading her arms wide like she was a model for *The Price Is Right*.

Claire rapid-blinked until her eyes adjusted to the white light that filled the airy studio, her heart fluttering slightly at the sight of it. She had avoided the studio at all costs since last year, when Alicia had ruined Claire's first day at OCD by painting her white pants with red paint period stain. Claire hadn't been back to the studio since, for fear of a panic-flashback.

The studio had been renovated at some point since Claire's fateful first day. Long slate tables had replaced the rows of easels and stools, and the walls and skylighted ceilings had all been painted a pristine white. At the front of the room a model in all black was hunched over his balled fist, frozen like a Rodin sculpture, while a kid in jeans and a worn gray T-shirt bobbed around him, taking his picture.

"What're we doing here?" Claire murmured, her eyes falling on a group of kids sitting cross-legged on the table in the back row. Some were sketching in spiral notebooks, and some were just hanging out, laughing and talking. A blond girl with fuchsia-dyed ends—Claire recognized her from study hall—was scowling into her iPhone camera, snapping a self-portrait.

Layne nodded at the SMART Board across the studio, where a boy with shoulder-length brown hair was scribbling something in shiny black marker:

WHEN I TAKE A PICTURE, I TAKE 10 PERCENT OF WHAT I SEE.

"Annie Leibovitz!" Claire blurted, then slapped her palm to her Blistex-buffed lips.

The guy turned around and grinned. "How'd you know?" He slipped a pair of retro black frames from his nose and cleaned the lenses on his T-shirt, which read TAKE YOUR BEST SHOT.

Claire flushed. "One of my favorites. It's on my Facebook profile."

"No way! Mine too."

"Claire, this is Iain," Layne announced proudly, licking sour crystals from her fingers. "He's the president of the Briarwood-OCD PC."

"The PC?" Claire muttered from the corner of her mouth.

"The Photography Club," Layne whispered back.

"Hey." Iain capped his marker and wiped his palms on his jeans.

The kids sitting cross-legged on the tables waved. Even the statue-still model at the front of the room cracked a smile.

Claire lifted her palm, wondering what Massie would say if she knew there was another PC at OCD. "Hey." Out of the corner of her eye, she noticed a collection of cameras on the table next to the door. There were tiny digital cameras, long-lens contraptions, and even an old-school pinhole camera. She hovered over them like they were velvet-cushioned diamonds in the display window at Cartier. Was that . . . No. It couldn't possibly be . . .

"The Nikon D90," Iain said behind her, reading her thoughts.

"OMG. I've never actually seen one in person!" she admitted.

"Wanna try it?" Iain grabbed the camera and planted it in Claire's hand. It felt solid and light at the same time, and the cool silver casing slid perfectly in her palm. "We bought a bunch of them. This one's an extra."

"An extra?" Claire choked, stroking the camera lovingly. "Don't these things cost a fortune?" She'd wanted to ask for one for Christmas, but when she'd Googled the price, she'd given up hope. That camera was worth more than Todd's life.

Iain shrugged. "The PC's got some pretty famous alumni that give money. Plus, we get to go to some of their gallery openings in the city and stuff."

"Food sucks, but the pictures are pretty good," laughed the girl with pink-tipped ends. "I'm Anya. Cool jeans." She slid off the table and joined Iain, Claire, and Layne at the back.

Claire glanced down at her faded Gap boot-cuts. "Seriously?" she said skeptically. Massie had docked her two whole points this morning for the hole in the left knee. It had brought her outfit rating down to a 7.6, which, as Massie had explained, was one-tenth of a point away from a mandatory bad sushi day.

But this PC was a different kind of PC. There wasn't a designer piece of clothing in sight, and no one had insulted her bangs, given her a once-over, or suggested she switch to the Sugar Busters diet to repair the damage she'd done on Halloween.

Was it possible that here she could just be . . . Claire— holey jeans, sweet tooth, and all? The thought alone made the knots in her shoulders start to dissolve.

"I thought you guys would . . . click," Layne joked, looking thrilled with herself.

The PC groaned. Anya pelted Layne with an empty film canister.

Claire giggled, a fresh burst of energy renewing her like a third helping of pomegranate Pinkberry. How could she have been at OCD for so long and not found these cool, artsy people who didn't care about clothes or ninth-graders? She swivel-turned toward Layne, lifting the camera. "Say cheeeese."

Layne stuck out her tongue.

Claire snapped the picture. "You're the best."

"I know," Layne beamed. "So I've got a Tween Inventors meeting in the auditorium in five. But wanna meet in the parking lot in an hour? My mom can give you a—"

Iain's iPhone buzzed in his back pocket. He checked the screen.

"Kelsey Morgan's walking the second floor with toilet paper on her shoe!" he yelled, stuffing his cell back in his pocket. "Time to move, people!"

The studio erupted into chaos. The rest of the PC leapt off the table, sprinting for the table of cameras next to Claire. She flattened herself against the back wall next to Layne.

"What's going on?" she yelled to no one in particular.

"A shot of the student body president with toilet paper on her shoe?" Anya slung a long-lens camera over her chest like she was a *National Geographic* photographer headed for the Serengeti on assignment. "That's gold, man."

"But . . ." Claire wrinkled her nose. Shooting girls with toilet paper on their shoes wasn't artistic. It was just . . . gross. "Why would the Photography Club—"

"Not the *Photography* Club," Anya clarified. "We're the Paparazzi Club! You coming?"

"Ummmm . . ." Claire took a step back. What was happening to the artsy, creative kids she'd just met? Were they just as shallow as the rest of OCD? Had she totally misjudged them?

"GO! GO! GO!" Iain boomed, tromping out the door behind

the PC without giving Claire a second look. The sound of the PC's footsteps faded down the hall.

Claire turned toward Layne, dumbfounded. Just minutes ago she'd had an image of a new OCD, an OCD full of fresh promise and possibility. But that image had blurred faster than an overexposed negative, leaving her feeling emptier than an old film canister.

Massie consulted the itinerary on her iPhone for the ninth time since the Range Rover had left OCD property. As long as Isaac didn't hit lunch-hour traffic or make any unauthorized stops, the PC were right on time. Even so, Massie refused to let herself relax. Her schedule that day was Botox-tight.

Itinerary: Ankle-Bird or Bust!!!

6:30 a.m.–6:42 a.m. Deep condition (Ouidad 12 Minute Deep Treatment Intensive Repair). No alpha should head into battle with stressed tresses.

6:42 a.m.–6:44 a.m. Text-remind Kristen to forge excused absence notes w/Layne's electronic Counter-Forge-It parent note signer.

6:42 a.m.–7:30 a.m. Blowout/makeup by Jakkob. Wardrobe: Alexander Wang leggings, Elizabeth and James Laurent shirt, Marc Jacobs snakeskin flats. (Note for PC: Nothing above a kitten heel, in case of need for speedy on-foot departure.)

7:30 a.m.–7:34 a.m. Range Rover, en route to Dylan's. GLOSS!!! (Glossip Girl Sweet Revenge Lip Stain)

7:34 a.m.–7:44 a.m. Meet PC in Couture Cemetery. Pick disguises so upgrades don't detect PC. SOMETHING SHINY to lure Ankle-Bird out of hiding (birds ♥ shiny things).

7:44 a.m.–7:52 a.m. Range Rover, en route to OCD. Review itinerary w/PC. Rate disguises. Hydrate/ energize (Red Bull Sugarfree).

7:52 a.m.–7:59 a.m. Give forged notes to Principal Burns. If she looks skeptical, compliment her hair on looking extra triangular today. Do NAWT laugh while saying it.

8:00 a.m.–12:20 p.m. Class. Whatevs.

12:20 p.m.–12:28 p.m. Range Rover, en route to ADD for "campus tour." Re-gloss as needed.

12:28 p.m.–1:02 p.m. HUNT DOWN ANKLE-BIRD!!!!!

1:10 p.m. Back to OCD. If time permits, victory lattes before 5th period.

"Four minutes out," Alicia called dutifully, reaching for the fitted gray Priorities blazer she'd draped over the black leather bench.

"Disguises on," Massie instructed. She re-glossed in less than five seconds, using the tinted divider between the front and back seats for a makeshift mirror. If she'd had any wiggle room in her schedule, she might have stopped to think about how weird it was that Claire had been so MIA for the past couple days. About how the window seat next to the fridge looked strange without the indent from Claire's Gap denim–covered butt. Or about how her most recent "gummy cramps" excuse was beyond transparent. But there just wasn't time. One slip-up and Ankle-Bird could fly the coop.

"What kind of bird was it again?" Kristen cinched the knot on her printed Pucci head scarf and adjusted her Tom Ford Samantha sunglasses.

"Hummingbird," Massie snapped. She tilted the air-conditioning vents in her direction and turned the air on full blast. The icy shot rippled through her tresses, sealing in the shine. As an added bonus, the air cooled her cheeks, which were flushed despite the slight autumn chill that nipped at the Range Rover's windows. All the planning had left her over-heated. Or was it nerves—and the thought of Landon catching her hunting Ankle-Bird in the off-season?

"Do guys in ninth like tattoos?" Dylan chewed her bottom lip. "'Cause my mom says if I ever get one, she'll cut off my clothes allowance."

"My mom says she'll homeschool me till college," Kristen grimaced.

"One of my Spanish cousins has a tattoo of angel wings on her lower back," Alicia offered, pulling a violet Patricia Underwood cloche over her ears. "It's kind of cool."

Dylan lifted her Red Bull Sugarfree can to her lips and tapped the bottom to get the last few drops. "Traaaaaaamp staaaaaaamp," she belched.

"Ewwwww." Alicia giggle-shooed away Dylan's burp fumes.

"The point is not whether the tattoo is quote-unquote 'cool'," Massie interrupted. "The point is that I am nawt letting some ink-stained ninth-grader steal my crush and cancel our upgrade." She looped her silver silk Diane von Furstenberg scarf around her head, careful not to ruin her blowout. "Are we clear?"

"Cuh-lear," the PC echoed.

"Good." As the Range Rover turned into the ADD front circle, Massie pulled her Gucci aviators from their protective case and cleaned them on the hem of her blouse. The Pretty Committee were suddenly silent. This was it. There was no turning back. She lowered her lids and conjured up a mental image of Landon's blue-green eyes. If this mission failed, mental images were all she'd have left. It was time to fight.

A light whirring sound filled the back seat as Isaac lowered the divider.

"Enjoy the informational interviews," he said, pulling up to the curb. "I'll be right here when you're done. And remember, it's always best to keep an open mind."

"Thanks, Isaac," the PC chimed, pursing their glossy lips together to keep from laughing.

Massie opened the door and lowered her black snakeskin flats onto the cracked sidewalk. Alicia, Dylan, and Kristen slid out behind her. Looking like a super-chic special-ops force on a top secret mission, the girls tiptoed across the crunchy, yellowed lawn. Massie tilted her face to the sky so the sun's bronzing rays could give her an extra boost.

When they reached the doors to the main building, Massie swiveled on the balls of her feet, facing her troops.

"Bathroom first," she whisper-ordered. "Then we'll hit the girls' locker room, the cafeteria, and the auditorium. Questions?"

"Ma'am, yes ma'am!" Dylan saluted, clicking her kitten heels together.

Massie rolled her eyes. "What, Dylan?"

"When are we gonna have time for lunch?"

Ehmagawd. How could Dylan possibly think about food, when the entire upgrade was in jeopardy? "No idea," Massie said impatiently. "Now. Are there any mission-related questions?"

The PC shook their heads. Dylan protest-clutched her stomach.

"Good. Now, let's go." With a determined flourish, Massie threw open the door and slid inside.

ADD's deserted main hallway smelled like a combination of old tuna fish and pencil erasers. Massie lifted her Chanel-spritzed wrist to her nose to stave off the odor. The chipped paint jobs on the lockers looked at least two semesters old, and the linoleum flooring was a dingy shade of brownish gray. She'd definitely do a better job appreciating OCD when she made it back. If she made it back.

"Ehmagawd, this lighting is the opposite of flattering," Alicia lifted her hand to shield her face from the flickering fluorescents overhead. "I am so nawt coming here," she announced, as if she'd actually been considering it.

The PC giggled behind their disguises.

Nearby, a girl in track shorts and a hoodie shoved a wrinkled dollar bill into a vending machine.

Massie glanced down at the girl's ankles. Apart from an ugly gold imitation anklet, the girl's ankles were free and clear.

"This place is, like, on the verge of collapse." Kristen hopped over a linoleum square that was curling up at the edges. "I don't know how the boys do it."

"Agreed," Massie nodded. The fact that Landon was rugged enough to withstand such hazardous learning conditions just made him hotter. She spotted the girls' bathroom at the end of the hall and motioned for the girls to pick up the pace.

"So then I'm like, 'Look, if you want to take a break, fine. Just don't expect me to be here when you've gotten blondes out of your system.'" A girl wearing low-rise jeans and a plaid men's shirt was leaning over the sink in the bathroom, applying thick, dark liner to her lids. A wallet chain dripped from her back pocket like a shiny snake. She didn't even turn when the Pretty Committee walked in. "I am so over high school boys."

"Right?" came a muffled voice from one of the stalls.

Kristen's eyebrows arched over the tops of her Fendi frames.

On any other day, Massie would have braved the hazy, Glade-scented bathroom to take notes on high school conversation topics for research. Today, she had more important things to do. She signal-nodded, and each member of the PC crouched in front of one of the four stalls.

Massie checked her stall: ripped gray denim rolled up at the cuffs and a scuffed pair of black Converse sneakers. No tattoo. Pressing her hands against her thighs, she pushed herself to standing and glanced at the other girls.

"Negative." Alicia shook her head, then stood up.

Kristen did the same.

Just then, the gray metal door leading to Dylan's stall swung open, smacking her in the forehead.

"Owwww!" Dylan toppled onto her butt, clutching her head in pain.

The Pretty Committee dissolved into giggles, their head scarves slipping.

A girl in a shapeless yellow sweater dress and flats peered out from the other side of the doorway. "What the—"

"Abort! Abort!" Massie squealed, checking the girl's ankles before she rushed out behind Alicia and Kristen. They stumbled into the hallway, doubled over.

"Ehmagawd," Alicia gasped, removing her sunglasses to wipe the tears from her eyes. "Did you see the look on that girl's face?"

The bathroom door flew open. Lips pursed tight, Dylan crossed her arms over her chest. A giant red welt was starting to form on her forehead. "Can we go now?" she grumbled, lifting her fingers gingerly to her rapidly swelling skin.

Massie shook her head. "We haven't even checked the cafeteria."

Kristen consulted her watch. "If we don't get out of here soon, we're gonna be late."

"If we each take five tables, it won't take long." Massie insisted. But her gloss, along with her resolve, was starting to fade. It had been more than seven hours since she'd chased her Dulce de Leche Luna Bar with a protein smoothie, and the fluorescent lighting and old tuna smell was starting to make her feel light-headed.

"Speaking of the cafeteria . . ." Dylan glanced down at her belly. It growled in response.

"If we check the cafeteria, the boys'll see us for sure," Alicia said warily.

"Fine. We'll check the locker rooms and then get out of here." Beneath her scarf, Massie's scalp was starting to sweat. Panicked, she fanned her hairline. Sweaty scalp led to oily tresses. Which led to breakouts. Which led to social isolation, which led to LBRdom. If she didn't find Ankle-Bird soon, she risked losing more than her crush. She risked losing her alpha status.

"I dunno." Kristen checked her watch again. "What if we get in trouble for being late and I lose my scholarshi—"

"The only thing making us late is your chitchat!" Massie

hissed. "Now come awn!" She charged past a faded yellow bulletin board sprouting flyers for the spring musical, the French club, and yearbook picture day.

Silently, the PC hurried alongside her, the buzzing fluorescent lights making them look more washed-out than the Olsen twins. No wonder ADD girls bronzed as often as Massie glossed.

"Anybody know any bird calls?" Kristen muttered at her navy flats. "That'd speed this thing up."

Massie pretended not to hear. Giving in to distractions could rob her of the element of surprise, giving Ankle-Bird the upper wing. The only option was to stay focused on the maroon doors at the end of the hallway, which were barricaded with piles of nylon gym bags. Bingo.

She kicked the gym bags out of the way when she reached the door. Once the path was clear, she handed out assignments.

"Leesh, you check the showers."

Alicia raised her left eyebrow. "Um . . . that's illegal."

Massie shrugged her off. "Then you and Dylan can split up the locker bays. Kristen, scope out the bathroom stalls. And I'll check the changing area. If you have a sighting, text ANKLBRD." She paused for a quick Purell break before flinging open the locker room doors. Immediately, the overpowering smell of sweat and ripe sneakers laced with fruity body spray rushed over her, yanking her stomach to the back of her throat.

"Yechhhh." Dylan pushed her sunglasses down her nose, pinning her nostrils together.

Scarves wilting and shades fogging from the sweat steam hovering in the air, the Pretty Committee barreled down the narrow, maroon-painted cinderblock hallway, which led to several empty rows of dented half-lockers. The only sound was the slow drip of a faucet somewhere nearby.

Massie's shoulders fell. "Where id eberybuddy?" she muttered, refusing to breathe through her nose.

"Comin' through." A muscular, ruddy-faced brunette wrapped in a threadbare mini-towel bowled past the PC's huddle, headed for a corner locker. Massie crossed her fingers. If this was Ankle-Bird, she could relax and call it a day.

Her eyes slid past the girl's it's-obviously-been-three-days-since-I-shaved knees. Around her left ankle was a bluish-black vine tattoo. But no bird.

"Doh-buddy's eben here," Dylan whisper-whined, blinking over the tops of her sunglasses. "Cad we just go back?"

Massie opened her mouth to reply, but was cut off by the thundering sound of soccer cleats tromping down the hall toward them. The Pretty Committee's eyes widened like deer in headlights. Before they could duck out of the way, a wall of uniform-clad, ponytailed soccer players rushed the lockers.

"Ahhhhhhhhh!" The Pretty Committee stumbled back on their flats as the sweat-drenched girls rushed by, threatening them with death by cleat.

"Ex-cuh-USE US!" Taking an elbow to the navel, Massie dove out of the way, colliding with the cold metal of the nearest locker. Ignoring the debilitating pain, she surveyed the passing ankles. They were all covered in shin guards and knee socks. What if the Ankle-Bird was trapped beneath an acrylic fabric cage?

Riiiiiiiiiiiiiiiiiiiing!

Even in the humid locker room, the clang of the ADD bell sent shivers down Massie's spine. Feeling woozy from the sweat stench and lack of breathable air, she nodded at the Pretty Committee to evacuate the premises.

"Okay, now can we go?" Kristen asked when they burst into the brimming hallway. She massaged her left shoulder and winced.

"Seriously!" Dylan shouted over the deafening roar in the halls. "I think I'm gonna faint!" She made a beeline down the hall for the vending machine near the front doors, extending her elbows to her sides so she could power her way through the crowd.

"Dylan!" Massie ripped off her sunglasses and shoved them in her tote, cradling it close to her torso. "We are nawt done here!" She stomped in Dylan's wake, ignoring the stares. Alicia and Kristen followed.

Dylan jammed a ten-dollar bill in the machine and pressed six different buttons. Seconds later, she was cradling a Dasani bottle and seven packs of neon orange cheese crackers. She deposited six packs into her purse and tore the last one open. She cracked the bottle open and downed half its contents in a single gulp. Then she went for the crackers.

"'Orry," she shrugged over a mouthful. "Low 'lood 'ugar."

"Okay, now we reeeeally have to go." Kristen bounced up and down like she hadn't peed in years.

Massie's jaw clenched. Maybe the other girls weren't ready to upgrade. This was the price she paid for being ten times more mature than the rest of her—

"Oops." A girl in skinny jeans and a shrunken leather blazer bumped into Massie on her way to the vending machine. A vanilla-colored envelope fell from her back pocket. A paw print was stamped on the back flap.

Massie froze. The paw print was exactly like the one on the invitation she'd seen Ankle-Bird give Landon in his room. Her head snapped toward the girl's denim-disguised ankles. Had fate intervened? Was this the girl she'd been looking for all along? There was only one way to find out.

She fake-stumbled into Dylan, sending the open Dasani bottle flying. It hit the linoleum floor, soaking the girl's feet.

"Ehmagawd, she is soooo sorry," Massie gushed, yanking Dylan's scarf out of her hair.

"Hey!" Dylan slapped her palm to the top of her head.

"No problem. Just water." The girl eyed Massie skeptically.

"No. Seriously." Massie knelt to the floor, patting the girl's feet dry. Lifting the hem of her jeans, she checked the ankles. Nothing.

"Um, you really don't have to do that." The girl was starting to look weirded out. She jammed her change into the vending machine, retrieved her snack, and hurried down the hall.

Defeated, Massie rose to her feet. "Not her."

"There has gawt to be an easier way to do this," Alicia

sighed, kicking the fallen envelope out of her path. It slid toward the gap underneath the vending machine.

Massie lowered her ballet flat onto the paw printed flap just in time. Then she crouched down and picked up the envelope, unfolding the invitation inside as carefully as if it were an ancient treasure map.

1st Annual
PUP-A-PALOOZA
Music Fest & Charity Auction
Hosted by the Abner Doubleday Day Kennel Club
WHO: You and your puppy!
WHERE: Westchester Dog Park
WHEN: Saturday, November 15th, 8 p.m.
WHY: 'Cause we ♥ to party with our puppies!!
FEATURING: Live music, complimentary pet spa services, an auction benefitting the Westchester Humane Society, and much, much, more . . .
** Regrets: Text "Pup-A-Pa-Loser" to 917.555.0817

The tension throbbing in Massie's body began to ease instantly. Maybe fate really had intervened. Now she knew exactly where to find her target. And if Ankle-Bird wouldn't come to her, well, then she'd go to Ankle-Bird.

Smiling into the four-way mirror in the sprawling BCBG dressing area, eight Massie Blocks tilted their heads to the right, examining the eleventh outfit of the afternoon: a rib-squeezing navy minidress with a sequined asymmetrical hem.

The original Massie snuck a shallow breath and admired her bronzed shoulders in the soft lighting. "Does this say 'ninth-grade charity benefit' or 'eighth-grade semiformal'?" She turned around to consult the Pretty Committee, who were lounging on the floor of the minimalist dressing room, balancing recharging triple-shot lattes on their knees. Glossy shopping bags brimming with expertly folded wardrobe options littered the gold carpet.

Alicia sat against one of the mirrored panels. She examined Massie with the solemn focus of a *Project Runway* guest judge. But before she could respond, her iPhone pulsed with a text. She lifted her left index finger, the way Kendra did when she was on a call.

"Aidan's going to Pup-A-Palooza too!" she announced, batting her lashes at the screen. "And he wants to know if I'm going!"

Massie jammed her hand on her hip. "Leesh. Benefit or semiformal?"

"Pluuuuus he wants to know if I'm bringing my puppy!" she squealed, slapping the soles of her black Pour La Victoire over-the-knee boots on the carpet.

"You don't have a puppy," Dylan reminded her.

"So? I'll get one." Alicia dipped into the reject pile next to her, lifting a moss-green spaghetti-strap gown and draping it over her skinny charcoal cords. The hazy green hue made her dark eyes gleam. "What kind of puppy goes with green silk?"

Kristen swatted Alicia's silk-covered thigh.

"Do you girls need help in here?" A smoky-eyed salesgirl in low-rise black pants and a purple silk tank popped her head into the dressing area. She eyed the pile of dresses on the floor with disdain. "You know, you're only allowed six items in the—"

"Do you have this one in a smaller size?" Alicia tossed the spaghetti-strap dress toward the doorway, obviously just trying to get the girl out of her hair.

"And this one!" Dylan balled up the ivory sheath and giggle-pitched it.

"Wait!" Kristen flung a bronze maxidress in the sheath's wake.

"I'll check," the girl sighed.

"So has Landon texted if he's going?" Dylan gulped her free-trade latte, then plunked her cardboard cup down at Massie's feet. A few drops leapt from the cup and soaked the puffy gold carpet fibers. Option number four, a cream one-shoulder sheath, was draped over a wingback chair by the doorway. Dylan yanked it free and used it to dab at the carpet stain.

Massie turned back toward her reflection in the mirror. "He hasn't decided yet," she lied, eyeing her silent, dark cell, which was nestled on top of her pumpkin Chloé Forever bag for easy retrieval. Her minidress was starting to feel tighter by the second, like she'd just hit the Cinnabon in the food court—hard. Why hadn't Landon called or text-invited her to the benefit? Were they nawt exclusive? Did he want to see other crushes?

"What if he takes Ankle-Bird?" Alicia wondered aloud. Then she slapped her palm over her mouth.

Massie narrowed her amber eyes at her friend.

"So how're you gonna find her Saturday night?" Dylan asked quickly.

"I don't know," Massie admitted, biting her lower lip. "I have to figure out a way to check all the ankles at the—"

"Luke's band's playing Saturday night!" Dylan cut Massie off, distracted by her cell. Then she nudged Alicia's thigh with the tip of her round-toe wedges and gasped, obviously forgetting about Massie's dilemma. "What if he asks me to hang backstage with the other rock-star crushes?"

"Opposite of fair!" Alicia pouted.

"Bring me!" Kristen begged.

Massie wanted to stomp her bare foot on the carpet as hard as she could, then demand that the girls focus on her for the rest of the afternoon. They seemed to have forgotten that if it weren't for her, they'd still be same-grading at soccer practice instead of upgrading at a benefit. She cleared her throat and tried one more time.

"Does this say, 'BE-NUH-FIT' or 'SEH-MEE-FOR-MAL'?" she blared.

Finally, the PC quieted, shifting their gazes in her direction.

"Neither." Dylan eyed the sequined hem. "It says, 'V-V-V-VEGAS, BABY!'"

Alicia and Kristen exploded into giggles, turning their attention back to their phones and texting like there was no tomorrow.

Massie whirled back around, taking a second look. Horrified, she realized that her friends were right. The sequins practically belted out showgirl, while the hem length suggested another Vegas-friendly occupation. She reached for her latte and chugged half its contents, braving the scorching pain that seared her throat. Was she losing it? Cracking under the pressure of finding the perfect charity auction–crashing outfit? Or had the expedition to ADD exhausted the fashion sense right out of her?

As she stared at the sequined BCBG monstrosity, she mentally inventoried all the possible disasters that could ensue if Landon showed up to Pup-A-Palooza with Ankle-Bird instead of Massie. For one thing, the entire ninth grade would know that she was crush-minus. And with Alicia, Dylan, and Kristen moving on to ninth-grade crushes, where would that leave Massie? Stuck hanging with Claire and Cam?

Massie grabbed her iPhone. It was time to take matters into her own hands.

Massie: Plans Sat. Nite? Bean & I r having movie nite if u want 2 join.

She tried to ignore the sinking feeling that came every time she thought about the fact that Landon had never even mentioned Pup-A-Palooza, let alone invited her. What was he trying to hide? She stared at the screen, willing it to buzz. It worked.

Landon: Can't. ☹ Dinner w/ the parents. Wish we could hang out tho . . . maybe Sunday?

Massie reread the last line six times, the words more affirming than a commission-driven salesgirl. Derrington and Dempsey never would have come right out and told her they wanted to hang out with her alone. But ninth-grade boys didn't play games. And neither would she, as soon as she found Ankle-Bird. As much as she hated the idea of showing up solo to her very first high school party, maybe things were better this way. With Landon MIA, she could focus 100 percent on the hunt for Ankle-Bird . . .

A freckled redhead in braided pigtails appeared in the doorway, holding a magenta tulle skirt.

"Occupied," Massie barked, without taking her eyes away from her phone.

"But . . ." Confused, the girl eyed the aisle of vacant white dressing cubes past the mirror.

"Save yourself the trouble," Kristen advised, slathering her lips with her new Smashbox gloss. "Not your color anyway."

In a huff of pink tulle, the girl stalked out of the dressing room.

"Ladies, I have an idea," Massie announced.

Kristen, Dylan, and Alicia turned to face her, and Massie was back where she belonged—in the spotlight. And after Massie dealt with Ankle-Bird, her upgrade would be complete—and just like her betas recognized her as their leader, Landon would realize there was no better crush, or animal supporter, than Massie Block.

"Me first." Layne hovered excitedly over the giant chrome eight ball bolted to a display stand at the front of Brookstone. Pressing her palms on both sides of the ball, she screwed her eyes shut. "Ummmm . . . willmeandDempseyenduptogether?"

Claire shook her head, plucking a green gummy from the waxy paper bag in her palm. "You know those things don't really work, right?" she asked glumly, releasing the gummy onto her outstretched tongue. But if she'd been alone, she would have asked the eight ball if she was doomed to live the rest of her middle school days in social purgatory, hovering on the outskirts of the Pretty Committee, with no new friends to show for the sacrifice.

And right now, it seemed like the eight ball's answer would be *No duh, Claire.* That's what she got for trying to branch out. Did she really think she could find better friends than the Pretty Committee? And did she think she could do it without hurting Massie's feelings?

"Shhhhh." Layne scrunched her features together, making her face look a little too much like Bean's. Claire was suddenly reminded of Massie's trip to ADD earlier that day. A terrifying thought forced its way into her mind: What if the PC had fallen so in love with high school, they'd decided to transfer, ay-sap? The gummy suddenly felt like lead on her tongue.

"The outcome is highly unlikely," bleated the eight ball's electronic robot voice.

Layne's eyes snapped open. "This one's busted," she informed a passing pimply-faced sales associate. "You should probably bring out a new one, um . . . Darrell," she said, squinting at the name tag pinned to the employee's polo shirt.

Darrell eyed the neon orange Doritos fingerprints on the side of the ball.

"Come on, Layne," Claire said quickly. "Let's go check out the karaoke machines."

She dragged her friend away from the eight ball, trying to shake the sinking, anxiety-filled, boulder-in-the-pit-of-her-stomach feeling that came on when she thought about the Pretty Committee's new ninth-focused lives. She reminded herself that if they could move on to bigger and better things, so could she. Only those bigger and better things would still be in eighth.

"Do you think Cam would use an alarm clock that wakes him up with a recording of my voice?" Claire paused in front of a neatly stacked display pyramid, standing on tiptoe to reach the box at the very top. "Or is that creepy?"

"Creeeeeeeeeeeeepy," breathed Darth Vader's voice from a pair of surround-sound speakers next to Claire.

"Look at this thing!" Layne gushed, waving a wireless mic over her head. "It has settings for, like, five hundred different character voices. Listen to this one." She programmed a number into the keypad on the mic and raised it to her lips.

"KUH-LAIRE."

Claire doubled over laughing at Layne's spot-on impression of Massie, backing into the display. The cardboard pyramid toppled to the floor as feedback from the mic squealed throughout the store.

Eeeeeeeeiiiiiiiiiiiiiiiiiiiiiiiiiiiiiiiiiiiiiiiiiiiiiiiiiiiiiiiiiiiiiiiiiiiiiiiiii!

"Ahhhhh!" Layne ditched the mic and plugged her ears.

An elderly woman eyeing a digital photo display next to her turned down her hearing aid and hobbled out of earshot.

"Ehmagawd!" Claire dropped to her knees amid the rubble, trying to restack the boxes. But she was laughing so hard, tears blurred her vision. The harder she laughed, the more the knot in the pit of her stomach seemed to loosen, leaving her feeling lighter. Like things were back to normal, and she didn't have to worry about upgrades or mining OCD for diamonds in the rough that apparently didn't exist.

When Claire finally wiped her tears away, the first thing to come into focus was a pair of black Marc Jacobs snakeskin flats. Claire knew those flats. And those flats meant one thing: Massie's voice had been the real deal. Claire's toes curled involuntarily, and she braced herself.

"Kuh-laire," Massie's voice echoed throughout the store again. Claire tilted her head back to get the full view. Massie was standing with one hand on her jutted hip, the other wrapped around a microphone. Tissue-stuffed bags from

BCBG, Sephora, Nordstrom, Club Monaco, and Bark Jacobs hung from her crooked elbow. Dylan, Kristen, and Alicia stood next to her, each with bags of their own. Posed in the middle of the alarm clocks and the digital photo display section, the girls looked like mannequins somebody had delivered to the wrong store.

"Oh. Hey." Claire swallowed a giggle, pushing herself to her feet. For some reason, she had the sudden itch to duck behind the globes display at the back of the store. Massie knew Claire and Layne were friends, and that they hung out without her sometimes. So why did Claire feel like she'd just gotten caught friend-cheating? "What're you guys doing here?"

"We're here on official business," Massie informed Claire briskly. "We need to talk to Layne."

Alicia, Dylan, and Kristen nod-agreed.

Claire narrowed her eyes at the countless bags dripping from the PC's arms. The only business they were in was that of overspending.

"Official business?" Layne cleared her throat and stepped forward, looking intrigued. "Follow me." She waded through the pile of alarm clocks, leading Massie and the PC deeper into the store. Claire scrambled after them, before Darrell the sales associate had a chance to see the rubble.

When they reached the back of the store, Layne nodded at Massie. "Step into my office," she said smoothly, motioning toward two caramel leather massage chairs with remote controls on the armrests.

"Ehmagawd, Layne." Massie looked annoyed, but she deposited all the bags (except the Bark Jacobs one) onto the carpeted floor and slid into the chair on the left.

Claire wrinkled her brow. What could Massie possibly need so badly that she was willing to take orders from Layne?

"Just a moment." Layne leaned over Massie's armrest, her fingers flying over the remote control. Then she did the same to her chair and plopped down next to Massie. Within seconds, rolling vibrations buzzed from the girls' heads to their feet, and back up again.

"Sooo telll meeee hoooow Iiii cannnn heeeeeeelp youuuu," Layne groaned, closing her eyes.

Alicia sighed loudly, leaning against a shelf of talking thermometers.

Kristen was bobbing her head to the beat of the tiny MP3 player/pedometer she'd lifted from a nearby display.

Massie's snakeskin flats bounced uncontrollably on her footrest. "Iiii neeeeed aaaa faaaaaaaaavorrrr," she purred, the delicate charm bracelet on her wrist jingling in time to her trembling voice. She reached into the gold Bark Jacobs bag in her lap and produced a tiny shoe box. She lifted the top and Layne peered inside.

"Baaaaaaby booooties?" The apples of Layne's cheeks shook in confusion.

Massie swung her head from side to side. "Doogggiiiieee boooooties."

"Ehmagawd, I opposite of have time for this." Alicia

stomped over to the chairs and dug her manicured nail into the OFF button on each remote. "The mall closes in, like, five hours and I still need a dress and a dog."

"Doggie booties," Massie repeated, sitting upright. She plucked a brown suede bootie from the box and dangled it in front of Layne's nose. "I need cameras installed in all of them." She wiggled against the buttery leather seat, scratching her back.

Layne examined the shoe carefully. "Bootie cams? Easy breezy," she said finally. "But it's gonna cost you."

"Given," Massie said happily. "You don't take AmEx, do you?" She reached for her purse.

Layne snorted. "I don't want your money," she said. "I want Dempsey."

Claire's eyes widened.

Massie's jaw dropped.

And Kristen flushed. "Layne. That's totally not fair," she protested, digging her toe into the gray carpet.

"What's the problem?" Layne shrugged. "You guys don't want him anymore, right?"

"Obv." Massie and Kristen speed-shook their heads a little too quickly.

"So then pinky-swear you won't ever crush on him again. AND you won't get in my way when I do." Layne planted her elbow between the leather armrests and extended her pinky.

Massie did the same. "Done, done, and done," she said quickly, gripping Layne's silver-ringed pinky in hers.

It was official: Claire had stepped into an alternate universe. A universe where Massie asked Layne for favors and Layne accepted payment in the form of ex-crushes. A universe where loving eighth automatically made you an outsider. The problem was, Claire couldn't decide which was worse: living in her old world, where she sometimes felt like the PC owned her soul, or living in her new one, where she felt like she didn't belong to anyone or anything.

When they slid out of the massage chairs, Massie and Layne were beaming. Claire couldn't tell if it was because of the massage or the fact that they both clearly thought they'd just gotten the better end of the deal.

"So what are you really doing here?" Claire asked Massie, nodding at the small mountain of colorful bags piled at the foot of the chairs. The floor of Brookstone looked like the Lyons' living room on Christmas morning.

"Shopping for a party Saturday night," Massie said, her voice measured. For a brief second, her amber eyes lit up. Was that hope? Worry? Anger?

Claire braced herself. "What kind of party?"

"A niiiinth-grade one," Alicia offered, giving the word *ninth* at least six syllables.

"Interested?" Massie plucked an envelope from her back pocket and handed it to Claire.

The thick, expensive paper felt heavy in Claire's palm. She opened the envelope, pulled out an invitation, and scanned it. "Pup-A-Palooza?"

"It's a charity auction," Dylan piped up, snapping open a

cellophane package of peanut butter crackers. "You bid on pet spa packages and outfits and stuff."

"You can even bid on some of the puppies from the local shelter," Kristen added. "And all the proceeds go to the Westchester Humane Society."

"And since I'm so into charity and animal rights . . ." Massie didn't bother finishing the sentence. "You can both come if you want," she said generously, side-glancing at Layne. "Since it's for a good cause."

Massie, Alicia, Dylan, and Kristen cocked their heads to the side, waiting for Claire and Layne to accept.

Claire hesitated, stifling the urge to funnel the rest of her gummy bag directly into her mouth. She needed the energy boost for what she was about to do.

"No thanks. I'm more into eighth-grade parties," she said calmly, even though her insides were screaming. The fresh-from-Orlando Claire would have jumped at the chance to do anything Massie wanted to do, no matter what. But that wasn't the case anymore. Claire didn't know exactly where she belonged these days, but she knew where she didn't: at a ninth-grade party.

Massie leaned forward slightly, like she hadn't heard Claire correctly. "But I picked a crush for you and everything," she said, sounding surprised.

"And he has two different lengths of hair!" Dylan added.

"Huh?" Layne looked confused.

Claire didn't bother trying to figure out what Dylan was talking about. She took a deep breath through her nose and looked directly at Massie.

"I already have a crush." She spoke slowly, like she was explaining algebra to a toddler. Or like she was explaining loyalty to an alpha. "His name is Cam."

Massie sucked in a sharp breath, her amber eyes flashing. "Big mistake, Kuh-laire."

"What is?" Claire snapped, all the confusion and guilt and sadness of the past few days morphing into anger. "Ditching your crushes for a bunch of boys you hardly know? Or wasting all your time spying on them?" She knew she was being harsh. But why should she hold back? She wasn't just fighting for herself. She was fighting for Cam, who was the one constant, steady presence in her social life. She was fighting for their relationship. And she was fighting for eighth.

"Claire, are you Heather Mills's bum leg?" Massie's voice was eerily calm, like the air in the seconds before a category five hit the Gulf Coast. She didn't even wait for Claire to respond. "'Cause you're totally dragging behind."

"Point," Alicia breathed.

Alicia's vote of confidence seemed to spur Massie on even more. "You can't stay stuck in eighth forever, Claire. Sooner or later you have to catch up with the rest of us."

"You should come." Kristen forced a smile. "It'll be fun."

"You have two choices, Claire." Massie's cheeks were starting to look like she'd triple-pinched them. "Either come to the party Saturday night—"

"Or what?" Claire cut her off boldly. "You'll ditch me, like you ditched your crushes?"

"Awww, snap," Layne muttered under her breath, taking a cautious step back.

"Did I say I'd ditch you?" Massie blinked, turning toward the PC.

Alicia, Dylan, and Kristen shook their heads.

"You didn't have to." Claire's mouth was starting to taste like pennies. "I know the drill."

"Good. Then we'll see you Saturday." Massie smiled wanly. Her gloss had long since evaporated. She swooped down and scooped up her bags. "I'll need those booties by Saturday, or the deal's off," she told Layne. Then she turned on the balls of her flats and marched out of the store. The rest of the girls followed.

Claire staggered backward into the nearest massage chair. Being friends with Massie took more dedication, hard work, and sweat than Gwen Stefani's flat abs, and required more sacrifices than a Dionysian ritual.

Layne shimmy-wedged herself into the chair next to Claire. The straining leather squeaked in protest. "Bummer," she said supportively.

Claire nodded miserably. "Maybe I should just go."

"I wonder if I could bring Dempsey as my date," Layne joked.

Claire cracked a smile. But it was a hollow one.

Layne was quiet for a while. Then she shifted onto her hip, facing Claire. "I have an idea," she said slowly. "You're not gonna love it, but just hear me out."

As Claire listened to Layne's plan, every cell in her body

was waving a white flag. She'd done everything in her power to fight for eighth. What more could she possibly do? But what if Layne's idea worked . . .

"Okay, I'm in," she said, reaching for the chair remote. She turned it on full blast, hoping the vibrations would shake the last ten minutes from her memory.

"Massie?" Kendra Block's voice came over the intercom next to Massie's bedroom door, interrupting the low, soothing sounds of her confidence CD on loop. "Layne's here to see you."

"Can you hear me now?" Layne's breathy cackle sounded like she was just millimeters from Massie's ear.

"Send her up." Jamming her thumb into the PAUSE button, Massie leapt off her bed and hurried to the door, feeling like it was Christmas morning and Layne was Santa Claus. Because Layne wasn't just delivering bootie cams. She was delivering a way for Massie to spy on every ankle at Pup-A-Palooza, guaranteeing an Ankle-Bird capture by the end of the night. Layne was delivering hope for Massie's future with Landon. And that was priceless.

When Massie opened the door, Layne bulldozed past, wearing a faded black trench coat, rainbow-striped tights, and glitter-flecked jellies. In the middle of Massie's pristine all-white bedroom, she looked like a deranged mental patient in the isolation ward.

"Special deliiiiiiiiiiivery," Layne announced, a wide, orange gloss–stained grin lighting up her face.

At the sound of voices, Bean padded out from Massie's

closet, took one look at Layne, and yelp-scampered back into hiding.

"You're late." Massie eyed the alarm clock on her bedside table.

"I was busy adding a little extra flair." Layne made a weird gurgling sound, almost like she was swallowing a laugh. "Free of charge. But if you don't want 'em . . ."

"I didn't say that." Massie said, as casually as possible. "So let's see." She crossed her arms over her black Design History sweater tunic to keep herself from bouncing with curiosity.

"In a minute." Layne slid up to the Massie and Bean mannequins in the middle of the bedroom. Massie's mannequin was wearing a satin olive-green cocktail dress accessorized with strappy metallic Manolos and tasteful Kenneth Jay Lane chandelier earrings. Bean's mannequin was naked, since Massie was holding out on the puppy.

"Isn't this kinda dressy for a dog park?" Layne reached for the mannequin.

"Don't!" Massie yelped, squinting at Layne's fingers for any hint of barbecue dust or crystallized sugar. Who knew where those fingers had been?

"I'm just wearing jeans," Layne announced, like Massie had asked.

You would, Massie thought.

"What's Claire wearing?" Massie pretended to examine the hem of the dress for rogue threads. She'd checked Claire's Twitter status four times since noon, but Claire hadn't mentioned her plans for the night. Still, it just didn't seem possible that Claire would actually choose to spend her Saturday night without the Pretty Committee.

"Dunno." Layne shifted in her jellies. "We haven't talked about it." She was obviously lying.

Massie glared at her. "Just show me the booties, Layne."

"Chill, Phil." Layne undid the sash on her trench and snapped it open. She held the bootie box under Massie's nose, lifting the top slowly.

Massie grabbed the box peered inside. "Ehmagawd."

"I KNOW!" Layne lifted the fashion atrocities from their box. She had hot-glued every neon dyed feather, cheap plastic jewel, and glitter bead in the tristate area to the chocolate suede booties. "They're groundbreaking. You can't even see the cameras."

Massie's mouth went completely dry. That kind of footwear did nawt belong in her bedroom. It belonged in the wardrobe department of Fashion Disasters on Ice.

"Layne!" she screeched, finally finding her voice. "No self-respecting puppy would ever wear these!"

Layne stage-pouted, her lips twitching slightly. "Sorry. No refunds."

Before Massie could protest, Layne flounced toward the door. "Later, gator," she called over her shoulder, slamming the door behind her.

Dumbfounded, Massie stared at the closed door. She should have known not to trust Layne.

Sensing that it was safe to reemerge, Bean appeared in

the closet doorway, blinking curiously at the brown box in Massie's hand.

Massie swallowed, pasting a giant faux grin on her face.

"Heyyyy, Bean," she cooed. "Ready to try on your new booties?" She knelt to the powder-scented carpet and inched slowly across it toward her puppy, not even caring that she was wearing out the knees of her brand-new gray skinny Citizens.

When Bean caught sight of the booties, a low growl escaped her throat. She backed up a few steps, a wary glint in her wet eyes.

"Puh-lease, Bean," Massie begged. "Wear them for me."

But the determination in Bean's glowing black eyes said that not even the Dog Whisperer could make her change her mind.

Somewhere deep, deep, deep down, Massie was proud of her puppy for having such discriminating taste. Still, she wished Bean would take a fashion hit for the team, just this once. Massie's entire plan to find Ankle-Bird at Pup-A-Palooza depended on it. Since the event was ahbviously pet-friendly, no one would think twice about Bean being there. And the "bootie cams," as Layne referred to them, would be at the perfect height to record the guests' ankles. Plus, Layne and that LBR Candy Corn had figured out a way to hack into the SnoopDawg Web site, so Massie could monitor the bootie cam feed from her iPhone. And once she caught sight of that hummingbird tattoo, all bets were off.

The plan was nothing short of genius. But it, and the

future of Massie and Landon's relationship, depended entirely on Bean, who had just scampered into Massie's closet.

"Fine," Massie called after her. "I guess I'll just have to sit at home like an LBR and wait for Landon and Ankle-Bird's wedding announcement in the Sunday *Times*."

Bean nudge-slammed the closet door behind her.

Massie did a face-plant into her carpet, moaning into the thick white fibers. Parenting was beyond stressful. No wonder Jon and Kate had cracked under the pressure.

She allowed herself a full five seconds of self-pity before righting herself again. There just had to be another way to make this work.

Bean barked indignantly from behind the closet door.

Bark! Massie giggled at her flash of inspiration. If she could get Bark Obama to wear the booties and go to the auction, she could still ankle-spy without Bean having to humiliate herself in public. She pulled her iPhone from her back pocket and leaned against the foot of her bed, feeling renewed and back on track.

Massie: Want me 2 pick up Bark? I can watch him if u have 2 go to dinner.

Landon: Not sure Bark = healed enough to move . . .

Massie had to take a gloss break to shake that one off. Landon obviously hadn't been worried about Ankle-Bird moving Bark. So what was the problem? After she'd applied a triple coat of Glossip Girl Thin Mintspiration gloss, she returned to her phone.

Massie: I'll take xtra good care of him. Pinky-swear.
B there in 10.

She powered off her iPhone before Landon could protest.

"Oops!" she giggle-pouted, tossing her cell onto the bed. "Battery died."

Operation: Ankle-Bird or Bust was back on track. And tonight, coming up empty-ankled was nawt an option.

CURRENT STATE OF THE UNION	
IN	**OUT**
Bootie cams	Cam Fisher
Ankle-Birds	Ankle boots
Spying-eye dogs	Seeing-eye dogs

Claire had been to the dog park with her parents and Todd for tons of Sunday-afternoon walks, eating ice cream and watching Westchester's population of wrinkly old men cheat at chess and backgammon. But the lush green lawn, with its mosaic wishing fountain and maple leaf canopy, had never looked like this before.

Colored Christmas lights were threaded through the changing leaves, making the treetops look like glowing galaxies. The picnic tables that usually edged the park had been replaced with long, rustic wooden buffet tables piled high with sushi, cheese plates, and desserts for the humans, and Kobe beef and frosted dog treats for the puppies. The fountain at the center of the park had been transformed into a bubbling dog Jacuzzi. And behind the fountain stretched a spotlit main stage, where a guy in ripped black jeans was doing a sound check.

But the biggest difference was the people. Instead of being surrounded by ninety-year-olds and their chess boards, Claire was surrounded by ninth-graders and their puppies. And she was starting to wish she'd texted in sick. After all the time she'd spend talking up eighth, how could she have let Layne talk her into this?

"So this is Mrs. Potts and Dancing Dish Number Three."

Layne slung her arms around the two girls on either side of her, looking more relaxed than Massie and Kendra after a ninety-minute couple's shiatsu. "We met at theater camp last year." The plate of dog bone–shaped sushi rolls in Layne's left hand was tilting dangerously toward the grass, like the *Titanic* in the final seconds before it went vertical. "Guys, this is Claire. She's in eighth with me."

"You can call me Syd for short," Mrs. Potts—a petite brunette in torn boyfriend jeans, vintage peep-toe wedges, and a low-cut emerald sweater—smile-nodded at Claire. "At least till opening night anyway." She was cradling a tiny white maltipoo in a black sweater tunic and puppy Uggs, or PUggs, as Massie called them.

"Cara," said the other girl, a willowy blonde in an eggplant-colored jacket, a low-cut tank top, and cowboy boots. She unhooked her thumbs from the belt loops of her jeans and grabbed a passing guy with an electric bass guitar slung across his chest. "And this is my boyfriend, Doug." She pulled the boy in and lip-kissed him, right there in front of everybody.

Mrs. Potts didn't even bat a lash.

Boyfriend? Not crush? Claire raised her barkarita glass to her lips and fake-sipped, not knowing whether to stare at the ground or watch Cara and Doug make out like it was no big deal.

"Hey. What's up?" Doug finally pulled away.

"Hey. Nothing." Claire fought the urge to finger-comb her bangs. How was Layne acting so . . . natural around an entire park full of lip-kissing high-schoolers?

The pressure of needing to find new friends ASAP was starting to tighten around Claire's midsection like a cinched leather belt after a gummy binge. Layne's ninth-grade Westchester Community Theater friends were her last hope. If she blew this, she'd be more than an LBR. She'd be a BFFLLBR (BFF-less Loser Beyond Repair). And that was way, way worse.

"So I gotta run." Doug tossed his suspiciously sun-kissed, potentially highlighted bangs away from his forehead before they settled back over his eyes. "We're on in five."

"Doug's band is opening tonight," Cara explained proudly. "Before the auction."

"Awesome." Layne dipped a sushi roll in mustard and crammed it in her mouth.

"Smells Like Uncle Hugh." Doug looked at Claire.

"Huh?" Claire froze. Had she forgotten deodorant again? There wasn't even a way to sneak a quick pit sniff.

"Smells Like Uncle Hugh," Doug repeated. "My band. We're like a mix between Radiohead and Shinedown, you know?"

"Totally," Claire nodded, even though she didn't.

While Doug and Cara lip-kissed goodbye like he was shipping off on a six-month deployment, Claire scoped out the park, looking for the PC. This event was practically the opposite of one of Massie's parties. Instead of stuffy tuxedoed waiters carrying sterling silver trays of catered mini-food, there were two buffet tables—one at human height and one at puppy height—and guests helped themselves. Instead of a DJ, there were a bunch of ninth-grade bands. And instead of designer gowns, everybody wore jeans. Girls and their cru—their boyfriends were actually talking to each other, instead of faking like they'd never met. Plus, there wasn't a parent in sight. Claire pulled out her phone, wondering if Cam could get out of spending the night at Josh's.

Claire: What r u up 2? Wanna hang @ a high-skl party?

Claire held her breath.

Cam: Already at Josh's. ☹
Cam: P.S. Don't fall for any 9th gradrs.

Claire blushed, even though no one was reading the text over her shoulder.

Claire: Not 2 worry. Wanna go downtown 2morrow? Gourmet Au Lait?
Cam: Def. ☺

An opening guitar chord echoed over the mic, and the entire dog park erupted in cheers and barks. Claire could feel the vibrations from the music and the crowd inching their way from her Keds all the way up her body.

"MythighgoesnumbwhenIpoo!" Syd yelled to Claire over the music, releasing her puppy to the grass.

Claire almost giggle-spat her drink. "What?" she yelled back, leaning closer.

"I said, the guy on drums is so cute!" Syd glanced down at the black lace bra that peeked out from beneath her slouchy sweater. But instead of yanking up her V-neck in embarrassment, the way Alicia would have done, she inched it down a little further.

Claire looked up at the stage, shielding her eyes from the bright, swinging spotlights. The blonde on drums looked weirdly familiar. How did she know that guy?

And then it hit her. It was Luke, Dylan's new and supposedly improved crush. The upgrade reminder made Claire's stomach churn.

Cara closed her eyes and rocked out on air drums to the beat of the music, not seeming to care if anybody was watching.

"Niiiice," Syd laughed. "Looks like all those hours in front of the mirror paid off."

"Please." Cara opened her eyes and grinned. "Like you don't do the same thing." She waved at a guy in skater shorts who was leading a Great Dane across the lawn.

"Nope." Syd shook her head. "I'm on lead vocals." She raised her glass to her lips like a microphone and pressed her index finger into her left ear. "Except usually, my mic is my flat iron."

"Ehmagawd, I do the same thing!" Claire shrieked, temporarily forgetting she wasn't supposed to say, *Ehmagawd*. But nobody seemed to care.

"ME TOO!" Layne winked at Claire, as if to say, *See?*

"But I only use full-length mirrors," Syd continued, bending over to pet a giant golden retriever that was drinking from the fountain. "Otherwise the choreography's a total waste."

"Exactly," Claire laughed, feeling the tension in her shoulders starting to loosen. If Massie ever found out about Claire's mirror-singing, she'd probably expel her from the PC, effective immediately. But with these girls, it was like Claire didn't have to filter everything she said. It felt more freeing than spending an entire weekend in sweats.

"Hey, have you ever thought about auditioning for one of the shows?" Cara smiled. "We're doing *Little Shop of Horrors* in the spring."

"Wouldn't she be an awesome Audrey?" Syd bobbed her head to the music.

"Seriously," Layne agreed, shoving up the sleeves of her gray elbow-patched hoodie.

"I can introduce you to the director, if you . . ." Cara's voice trailed off. She was staring over Claire's left shoulder, her arched brow crinkling slowly in confusion. Claire turned around.

Behind her, the Pretty Committee were standing shoulder to shoulder in full hair and makeup, cocktail dresses, and heels that were sinking slowly in the grass like it was quicksand. At one of the Blocks' events, the girls would have looked photo shoot–chic. But in the middle of the dog park, they just looked overdressed and out of place. It was like seeing the cast of *Gossip Girl* in the frozen food aisle at the grocery store.

"Kuh-laire! You came!" Massie's amber eyes glowed excitedly under the colored lights, complimenting her single-strap olive-green satin dress. Bark Obama was tucked underneath her arm like a furry black clutch, lapping Kobe beef out of her upturned palm. "In Keds, but still." A Frisbee whizzed over her head, but her sculpted updo stayed frozen in place.

"Yup," Claire smiled, deciding to ignore the dis. Ninth-graders probably let it go when their friends insulted their footwear. Plus, as weird as it was to admit, Massie hating on her shoes felt comfortable, somehow. Familiar. "Massie, this is Syd and Cara."

"I think the Keds are adorable." Syd adjusted her bra strap. "Totally retro."

Then again, ninth-graders not hating on her shoes felt like a blast of fresh air. Claire bit the inside of her cheek to keep from smiling. Cam would probably like these girls way better than he liked the PC. Maybe she should text him again, just to see if—

"Puh-lease." Massie placed Bark gingerly on the grass with a fresh slab of beef. "Marc Jacobs's patent ankle booties are retro." She wrinkled her nose at Claire's feet. "Those things are just old." She lifted her palm in the air.

"Point," Alicia groaned, wresting her satin-covered heel from the ground. When she finally freed it, a chunk of dirt went flying through the air toward Cara, who had to duck out of the way.

"Oops," Alicia said coolly.

Cara rolled her eyes.

Massie's palm was still raised, like she expected the ninth-grade girls to slap it. But after a full five seconds in midair, it was obvious they weren't going to. Massie's eyes widened slightly, and she whipped toward the PC for help. But Dylan was too busy shoveling three wedges of cheese in her mouth to notice, and Kristen was kneeling in her silver sheath dress, petting Bark. Claire cringed, contemplating high-fiving Massie herself. Seeing them this overdressed was painful enough, even if they didn't seem to mind. But this . . . this was brutal.

"Leesh," Massie whisper-hissed through her uber-glossed smile.

"What?" Alicia was blending a dab of bronzed body shimmer into her shoulder. "Oh. Right." She lifted her palm and smacked Massie's about seven seconds too late.

Cara and Syd looked bored.

Layne snorted. "Speaking of mind-blowingly AWESOME shoes . . ." She grin-winked at Claire, nodding at the booties on Bark Obama's feet. The decorations were starting to come unglued, leaving a glittering trail in Bark's wake.

"Seriously?" Cara burst out laughing, kneeling down to inspect the booties. "What are these things?"

Massie reddened, her hand shooting into her cracked metallic clutch and emerging with her iPhone. Her fingers flew over the keys and she squinted at it intently, like it might levitate if she stared hard enough.

Claire lifted her glass to her lips again, to cover her twitching lips. It wasn't that she enjoyed watching Massie squirm. It was that she loved Massie seeing how Claire could hang with ninth-graders too, if she wanted to. And strangely enough, as she watched Cara inserting a fallen feather from Bark's booties into her jacket lapel, she was starting to think she did. Maybe age really was nothing but a number.

"So when'd you get here?" she asked, trying to capture Massie's attention. What she was really saying was *I'm here. Happy?*

"Just now," Massie murmured, glaring at the image of Syd's and Cara's ankles filling her screen. After a moment she dropped her cell back in her bag and turned her attention to Claire. "Having fun?" The glint in her jet black liquid-lined eyes said, *I knew you'd come.*

Claire nodded, turning away from the group. "Actually, these girls are really cool," she whispered, shielding her mouth with her empty glass.

"OMG, did I nawt tell you?" Massie whisper-giggled back, temporarily forgetting her own N-OMG rule.

"Tell her what?" Dylan elbowed her way into the powwow, her breath smelling like sharp cheddar. Her shiny red mane had been teased and tousled to new heights.

"About how ninth-graders are ten times better than eighth-grade LBRs," Massie beamed, hip-bumping Claire and looping her bronzed arm around her shoulder.

"Yup." Dylan was staring openmouthed at her new crush drumming away on stage, a cheddar crumb perched on her bottom lip.

"Fine. You told me," Claire admitted, basking in the glow of the old Massie. The Massie who said OMG, and took a break from crush-spying to giggle with her friends. Even if they were in eighth.

"Woooooooooo-hooooooooooooo!" shrieked the crowd as the band finished their set.

"Thanks, guys." Doug leaned into the mic. "We're Smells Like Uncle Hugh, and that song was called Pee-Hugh. We're gonna take a quick break, but stick around, 'cause we'll be back for more in just a few."

"Ow-owwww!" hooted someone in the crowd.

Somebody's dog barked in agreement.

Dylan's head snapped toward Massie. Her emerald eyes were panic-glazed. "Does my hair look okay? Should I go over there or wait for him to come over here?"

"Wait," Massie advised. "You don't want him to think you're desperate." She gripped Claire's wrist. Her hand smelled like beef. "Plus, that'll give us time to introduce Claire to her new crush."

Syd and Cara's eyes lit up at the exact same time.

"New crush?" Syd elbow-nudged Claire.

Claire shook her head, pulling away from Massie. "No thanks. I'm good." A sinking feeling in the pit of her stomach told her things were about to get uglier than Layne's home-made hoodie.

"Um, Kuh-laire?" Massie turned around, her grip tightening. "Are you Joan Rivers's face?"

Claire sighed. Massie cutting her down in front of the

ninth-grade girls was getting kind of old. "No. But I don't want a new—"

"Then why are you so frozen?" Massie snapped, her good mood evaporating faster than cheap moisturizer. Bark was doubled over on the ground in a coughing fit, but Massie ignored him.

"I told you already." Claire was starting to feel like a broken record. "I don't. Want. A new. Crush. I'm sticking with Cam."

Syd, Cara, and Layne were suddenly silent. Claire felt her cheeks getting hotter by the second. And it wasn't from the spotlights. As far as she was concerned, Cam *was* her upgrade. And she was sick of Massie acting like he wasn't good enough.

"Fine." Massie's jawline jutted out, and her amber eyes darkened. Claire had only seen that look of angry humiliation once before, when Kendra had taken away Massie's AmEx right in front of the PC for online ordering their fall wardrobes with her card because it was easier than entering five different card numbers, security codes, and expiration dates.

"Come on, Bark," Massie hissed, pivoting on her sinking heel.

Still wheezing for breath, Bark bent over Massie's foot and hacked up a neon blue feather.

"Ewwwww." Alicia giggled.

Lifting her chin slightly, Massie clenched her jaw and hobbled into the crowd. Bark limp-trotted behind her, followed by the rest of the Pretty Committee.

"What's with her?" Syd murmured to Cara.

Cara looking to Claire, her gray eyes questioning. But Claire just shook her head, too exhausted to bother explaining. Not that there was much to tell. It was pretty simple. Her friendship with the Pretty Committee was like Bark Obama's booties: coming apart at the seams.

Zigzagging through the underdressed crowd, Massie pinky-swore to herself not to let Claire take up one ounce of her mental energy until her mission was complete. Ankle-Bird was priority number one. And Massie was going to track her down the same way she'd tracked down the new Bottega Veneta metallic leather tote the day it had debuted at Saks: with focus, dedication, and a refusal to let a bunch of girls and their puppy-stuffed handbags get in her way.

"She's gawt to be here somewhere," Massie muttered to her cell. With one hand on her iPhone and the other pulling pieces of Kobe beef from the stash in her clutch, she cut across the grass, leading Bark toward the back of the park.

"Is it time for a break?" Dylan huffed in Massie's left ear, temporarily replacing the delicate notes of Chanel No. 19 that orbited her with the hot stench of blue cheese. "I wanna wish Luke good luck."

"Nawt yet." Massie recalculated her plan of attack. She'd work her way from the buffet tables toward the tiny massage tables where puppies were getting complimentary spa services, past the pockets of guests and their dogs stretched out on picnic blankets, around the Jacuzzi fountain, and up to the stage. And then she'd get Bark back to the Block Estate before Landon could flirt-thank her for all her help.

"Have you guys seen Scott yet?" Kristen shielded her eyes with her palm, scanning the crowd.

"Aidan texted and said he'd be here in five." Alicia snapped her picture with her cell, then studied the shot for imperfections.

"I should at least say hi before the band starts up again, right?" Dylan gripped her tiered black satin dress with both hands, taking long strides to keep up. "I mean, I want Luke to see me while my hair still looks good."

"Listen." Massie spun around to face the PC. "We're not here to find your crushes. We're here to find Ankle-Bird and leave, ay-sap." Her tightly wound chignon was starting to loosen, just like her grip on the evening. Feeling Bark's scratchy pink tongue flick across her fingertips, she reached for another piece of beef and refocused on her cell. Last year's Pumas, a pair of individual-toed rainbow socks, and a tiny Tinkerbell tattoo crossed the screen. But no hummingbird.

"ATTENTION." Kristen cupped her hands around her lip gloss–lacquered pout like a megaphone. "PUT DOWN THE SP-IPHONE AND STEP AWAY FROM THE BEEF. IT'S TIME TO PAR-TAY."

Alicia giggle-eyed the madras picnic blanket at her feet, where a girl and her crush were gunning for a Best Lip Kiss VMA.

"Be right back." Dylan shot toward the buffet like the

sushi rolls were tiny, powerful magnets and she was made of solid aluminum.

"Fine," Massie snapped, sick of the distractions. "Go ahead. Alicia, since Aidan isn't here, you can come with me. Watch the camera while I feed Bark." She thrust her phone into Alicia's hands.

"'Kay." Alicia took it, too busy staring at the lip-locked couple to protest.

"Meet at the fountain in twenty," she instructed the girls. "Come awn, Leesh." Stepping over a huddle of King Charles spaniels sharing a plate of chocolate-frosted pup-cakes, she lifted herself to the balls of her feet to keep her heels from sinking into the grass. Her shea butter–moisturized calves were already starting to burn. An outdoor charity event packed with puppies was like a six-inch Jimmy Choo heel: adorable in theory, but impossible to walk in.

Winding around the buffet table, she dropped tiny beef bits at her heels to keep Bark moving while Alicia followed behind. The bright lights, the buzzing and barking crowd, and the opening beats of the band on stage seemed muted, like she was walking underwater. Drifting mindlessly through the crowd, she tried to barricade her brain against thoughts of Claire. But it was pointless. Her mind was working in overdrive, trying to understand. Claire had practically been the mascot for eighth, and here she was ditching the PC for a pair of ninth-graders she barely knew? It just didn't make sense. Unless . . .

An earsplitting drum solo boomed over the loudspeakers, temporarily blocking the thought from Massie's mind. But the second the drums faded, it was back again, nipping at her heart just like Bark was nipping at her empty fingertips.

Maybe it wasn't that Claire cared about upgrading from eighth. Maybe she just wanted to upgrade from the Pretty Committee. Maybe she—

A cool breeze tickled her fingers where Bark's tongue had been, bringing her back. Her head snapped toward her feet.

Bark was gone.

"OMG!" She whirled around, smacking into Alicia, who was bent over the iPhone. "Where's Bark?"

"Ow!" Alicia rubbed her forehead, her dark chocolate eyes widening in pain. "Also? You're not supposed to say 'OMG,' remem—"

"Not the point!" Massie snatched the iPhone from her friend's open palm, her head throbbing. "Obama's MIA!" The pounding in her skull felt like one of Jakkob's soothing scalp massages compared to the stabbing pain in her heart. If anything happened to Bark, Massie and Landon would be done, done, and done-er. And losing Claire and her crush at the same time would be ten times more devastating than losing her AmEx privileges. Besides, what good was limitless credit when you didn't have a crush or friends to buy things for?

"Maybe he went to the Jacuzzi. For his foot." Alicia took charge, shifting seamlessly into broadcast journalist moment-of-crisis mode. "We'll check there, then double back to the massage tables." With a confident hair toss, she dipped in front of Massie and led the way toward the fountain. "He can't be that far. He's practically crippled."

Because of me, Massie reminded herself miserably. She followed, keeping her eyes on the camera feed for any clue as to Bark's location. But all she saw was a sea of poorly accessorized ankles, plus the occasional puppy butt.

"Negative." Alicia shook her head when they reached the Jacuzzi. Puppies on rafts and in water wings were bobbing in the churning water while their owners chatted and sipped drinks around the fountain's edge.

Massie's chest was starting to feel tighter than her cocktail dress. What if she never found Bark? What if Landon had her arrested for dog-napping? She couldn't go to jail! Who would take care of Bean? And what would happen to her Glossip Girl collection?

Suddenly, a fuzzy image of a hummingbird, hovering between a distressed pair of tan round-toe booties and dark-wash skinny jeans, lit up her screen—and her heart.

"EHMAGAWD!" Massie squealed, wanting to lip-kiss her phone right then and there. "LEESH!"

Alicia whipped around, her glossy black locks soaring over her shoulder like she was shooting a print ad for Frederic Fekkai. "What?"

"We got her!" A spotlight swung across Ankle-Bird's leg, giving away her location. "She's standing next to the stage!"

Her hope-battery recharged, Massie linked arms with Alicia and tromped toward the stage, closing in on Ankle-Bird with every step. Relief pulsed through her with the thumping beat of the band on stage. Together, the girls bobbed and weaved through the swaying crowd, pushing past girls taking shots of the band with their cells and guys slinging arms around their crushes. Massie kept her eyes on the ground, scanning the ankles closest to the stage. In the front row, she spotted her target. Bracing herself, Massie let her eyes travel from the ankles upward.

Alicia's jaw dropped. "Ehma—"

"Hawt," Massie finished. Ankle-Bird was standing right next to the stage, cuddling Bark and swaying effortlessly to the beat. Over her ripped skinny jeans, she wore a slinky teal tunic and a textured leather jacket. Long, perfectly tousled black waves tumbled past her boobs, screaming, *Yes, this is natural, frizz-free curl! And no, I don't even OWN a diffuser!* Her smoky eye makeup made her icy blue eyes pop. She was like the high school version of Sarah Jessica Parker: without the hair, makeup, and wardrobe, she probably wouldn't have been a threat. But the total package was a ten. Times ten. With one exception: She smelled like liver.

Massie's hand flew to her professionally sculpted bun, which was deflating faster than her ego. She'd give her right heel for a mirror, some gloss, and a hit of her confidence CD. But there was no time.

"Bark!" She forced herself to giggle-yell over the music, throwing her arms wide. "There you are! We were so worried!" She leveled her eyes at Ankle-Bird, to prove she wasn't the least bit concerned. Or threatened.

Alicia finally closed her mouth.

Ankle-Bird looked up, her smudged-to-perfection eyes crinkling in confusion. "Um, who're you?" she shouted.

Bark took one look at Massie and burrowed his face into Ankle-Bird's left boob.

Massie swallowed her hurt and slid her arms around Bark's pudgy middle. "I'm watching Bark for the night," she said, tugging at the puppy.

"Sorry." Ankle-Bird held firm. "I didn't catch your name," she said. Her nude-glossed lips looked even poutier close up.

"Does it matter?" Massie snapped. "This is nawt your dog." She gripped Bark's midsection and prepared to fight.

"No, it's MY dog!" shouted a familiar voice as the music on stage subsided and the crowd erupted into cheers.

Massie's heart seized like she'd just downed a double bacon cheeseburger.

"Crush alert," Alicia whisper-hissed, thirty seconds too late.

Landon stepped out from behind the stage, looking more adorable—and angrier—than Massie had ever seen him look. His single cheek dimple disappeared the second his blue eyes landed on Massie, as if it were punishing her by hiding.

"What are you doing here, Massie?" Landon asked as the noise from the crowd started to die down.

"What am I doing here?" Massie repeated, racking her brain for possible excuses. She'd heard music therapy was good for busted puppy paws? Dylan dragged her here for the free food? Alicia was doing a story on the party for Channel Five, and Massie was the only one who knew how to hold her cue cards at the right angle? "What are *you* doing here?" she deflected.

"We finished dinner early, and I went to your house to find you." Landon yanked up the sleeves on his charcoal Armani jeans sweater. "Isaac said you were here."

Under any other circumstances, Massie would have lip-kissed Landon right then and there for making such a romantic gesture. But from the stormy look in Landon's Caribbean blue eyes, now was not the time.

Before Massie could think of what to say next, a hot pink jewel from Bark's bootie landed on the toe of Landon's sneakers. "And what did you put on his feet?" he asked, tugging lightly at the toes.

Bark howled in pain. Masse crossed her arms over her chest. Bark was obviously exaggerating. He'd run to Ankle-Bird just fine.

"And now we're gonna take a break from the tunes," yelled the lead singer on stage. "The first auction item of the night has been donated by Bark Jacobs boutique."

The crowd went crazier than a pack of hobo-happy shoppers at a Kooba sample sale.

Ankle-Bird handed Bark over to Landon. "So I'll see you tomorrow at noon?" she asked, shake-tousling her curls and sending a fresh wave of liver scent through the air. Massie wrinkled her nose. "Your house?"

"You got a date." Landon's wink sliced through Massie's heart, and she staggered backwards into Alicia, who side-hugged her protectively. The sweet notes of Alicia's Angel perfume suddenly made Massie want to bury her face in her friend's shoulder and sob.

Ankle-Bird blew Landon a kiss, planted on one Bark's head, and ducked into the crowd without even giving Massie or Alicia a second glance.

"I gotta go." Landon shook his head, gingerly stroking Bark's foot. "Later." He turned and disappeared into the crowd.

Massie body felt as numb as Kendra's face after a marathon round of Botox. All she wanted was to curl up with Bean in her bed and forget about Landon, Bark, Ankle-Bird, and Layne's unthinkable taste in canine footwear.

"Wanna call the girls and Isaac?" Alicia asked softly, her eyes softening in pity. That made Massie want to cry even more. So she just nodded and stared down at her iPhone. Just as she was about to four-way call the rest of the PC, her battery icon flashed, and the screen went black. Massie blinked back tears as the crowd cheered for the start of the auction.

But unless someone was selling an unbroken heart, she wasn't interested.

The next morning, Massie's iPhone was the only thing that had been recharged. She'd tried all the usual confidence-boosting remedies: an emergency in-home highlighting session with Jakkob, Jacuzzi time with Bean, and falling asleep to her confidence CD. But she still felt emptier than a used Starbucks cup.

Cuddling her puppy to shield her from the afternoon chill, Massie knelt behind the barricade of holly bushes that separated Landon's property from the house next door. Through the prickly leaves, she surveyed the three-story brick house for any signs of predate movement, cursing Landon's mom for her landscaping choices. Why couldn't she have planted bushes in front of the house, so Massie could have a full-on view?

For a second, she wondered if she should have invited the Pretty Committee along, so one of the girls could have staked out the other side of the house. But the girls had been so into their new crushes at the party, they hadn't even taken the time to ask about Ankle-Bird.

If the PC had been there, they would have rated Massie's outfit a solid 9.75. Since she was alone, it had been up to Bean to *yap*-prove the burgundy silk Geren Ford tunic Massie had chosen to help her blend noiselessly into the piles of autumn leaves outside Landon's house. The tunic was a perfect match for her soft-as-cashmere DL 1961 boyfriend jeans, which ensured comfort for endless hours of spying on Landon's date with Ankle-Bird. And her tan suede boots would keep her feet warm, even if her heart felt frozen solid.

"What do you think he's doing in there to get ready?" she whispered to Bean, wondering if one of the side windows led to Landon's room. Was he re-spritzing CK Eternity Summer? Deciding between Puma and Prada? Flossing, in case of a lip kiss? The possibilities were heartbreaking.

Massie's iPhone lit up on the ground next to her. Slapping the crunchy leaf blanket beneath her, she kept her eyes trained on the house, then lifted the phone to eye-height.

Kristen: Where'd u go last nite? Me & D went backstage w/the band. Guess who's a total groupie now?

Backstage? Before Massie could come up with something ten times more alpha than backstage passes at Pup-A-Palooza, her cell buzzed again.

Dylan: Am nawt! ☺ P.S. Luke's giving me drum lessons 2morrow after skl. Don't need a ride home.

The comforting thump of Bean's heart through her matching burgundy cowl-neck made Massie feel a little less alone. Still, she'd never been on a stakeout without the PC before.

It felt sort of like going into a dressing room by herself. Being with the PC was half the point and most of the fun. But last night she'd gotten the message loud and clear: Her friends were way more interested in their upgrades than in keeping an eye on Massie's. So this time, she'd have to spy solo.

Bean wiggled free of Massie's grip and settled in a tiny bed of leaves next to her knees. Massie closed the text message, then reevaluated Ankle-Bird's OWCH (Older Woman Crush Hijacker) potential. Massie had to rate her at least an 8 out of 10. She had style and the perfect smoky eyes, and Bark was lapping out of her manicured hand.

A shiver ran from Massie's toes to her tunic, but it wasn't from the fall breeze that swept through the yard. An 8 out of 10 OWCH rating made Ankle-Bird a definite relationship terrorist. Threat level: orange. The only thing keeping her from being a full-on red alert was her eau de liver scent.

The muted thump of a drum beat cut through Massie's reverie and made Bean jolt into position. A low growl leaked from the puppy's throat as the smooth sound of a car engine sliced through the chilly air.

"Ehmagawd. It's time." Thrusting her hand into her Fendi Spy bag, Massie whipped out her newly upgraded Gucci shades and inspected them carefully. She'd rush-ordered the glasses from Layne, who had inserted mirrored binocular lenses into the sleek frames. After last night's bootie cam disaster, Layne had agreed to provide the service pro bono. And now, Massie was free to Ankle-Bird–watch at three hundred times the usual magnification.

At the far end of the drive, a silver MINI Cooper convertible appeared, coasting toward the house to the beat of the latest Killers song. Even though it was cold outside, the top was down. Ankle-Bird's shiny black locks whipped in the breeze, framing her face perfectly without getting stuck in her gloss. Mouth slightly parted, Massie plucked a sticky strand of her hair from her bottom lip.

The MINI Cooper eased around the front circle and came to a stop. There was nothing in the passenger's seat but a studded bronze tote, which meant Ankle-Bird's license wasn't her learner's.

A real driver's license, an ah-dorable car, and hair that practically defied the laws of physics? OWCH upgrade: 9.5. Threat level: red. Liver and all. A flood of insecurity filled the void in Massie's heart.

Ankle-Bird slid the keys out of the ignition, silencing the music. The driver's side door swept open, and she planted a teal round-toe wedge boot on the cement. A tiered bright yellow sweater dress swung around her knees, proving that she wasn't one to shy away from color. Massie rolled her eyes. Ankle-Bird *would* choose canary yellow. A slouchy leather belt accented her slim hips without stealing the focus from her face.

Massie shoved her sunglasses on, leaning forward to get a better view. Through the magnified lenses, all she could see now was Ankle-Bird's T-zone. Matte, poreless, and porcelain. The insecurity flood was turning into a tsunami.

Bean lick-assured Massie's denim-covered thigh. But the

glint in her tiny black eyes said she was dying for a ride in the passenger's seat of a silver convertible.

Massie tossed the glasses on the ground next to her and watched Ankle-Bird saunter up the brick front walkway to the navy-painted wooden front door. No last-minute cheek-pinching for color or BFF-texting for courage. It was like the girl didn't even care what Landon thought about her.

Without the slightest hesitation, Ankle-Bird gripped the brass door handle and let herself in. Massie bounced on her knees, craning her neck to catch a glimpse of Landon. But all she saw was the navy door slamming shut, making Massie more of an outsider than she'd ever been in her life.

An hour later, while Bean napped in the bed of leaves next to her, Massie was thanking Gawd that her iPhone had Internet capabilities. Imagining Landon, Ankle-Bird, and Bark together inside was like imagining her parents lip-kissing: too horrible to consider. So she hadn't. Instead, she'd indulged with some online retail therapy to numb the pain in her heart. If she couldn't have Landon, there was always Lanvin.

Bean let out a tiny, defeated snore. Stroking her puppy's warm ears for comfort, Massie checked the clock on her cell for the billionth time. Maybe she should just give up and take Bean home. After all, her heart wasn't the only part of her that was numb: She'd lost feeling in her fingertips somewhere between ShopStyle.com and CoutureCandy.com.

Just then, Landon's front door swung open and Ankle-Bird

emerged, with Bark at the end of a Burberry leash. With slow, pained steps, Bark inched his way down the brick walkway, whimpering under his breath. Ankle-Bird bent down and massaged Bark's paw, murmuring something under her breath.

"Ehmagawd, Bean," Massie whisper-snapped. "Bark's more of a drama queen than Layne."

Bean's eyes fluttered open at the sound of her crush's name. When she saw Bark, she leapt up and tried to bolt for the driveway. Massie gripped her by the cashmere cowl-neck and pulled her back into hiding.

As Ankle-Bird led Bark down the driveway, Massie stared at the front door, waiting for Landon to emerge. Where was he? And where was Ankle-Bird going without him?

Bean bared her professionally whitened canines, obviously wondering the same thing.

"Only one way to find out," Massie said, pushing herself to her feet. The tingling feeling in her boots was partly because she'd been sitting on her feet for the past hour. But it was partly from fear too. Not knowing what Ankle-Bird was up to was like not finding out you'd tucked your corduroy mini into your tights until last period: Being in the dark was humiliating, but finally finding out the truth was humiliating squared.

Massie shook the tingling feeling from her feet one at a time, brushed away the leaves smashed to her butt, and got ready to follow that bird.

The second Ankle-Bird and Bark turned onto the road, Massie scooped up her puppy and tiptoed across the leaf-strewn lawn, hot on the trail. The sound of Bean's excited panting in her ear spurred Massie on in her quest for the truth. Landon Crane was her most adorable, stylish, mature crush yet. And she wasn't going to let him go without a fight. Even if it was a totally unfair fight, with MINI Cooper convertibles and naturally frizz-free hair involved.

When Massie and Bean veered onto the maple-lined street, Ankle-Bird and Bark were only a few steps ahead, since Bark's drama limp was slowing him down more than complex carbs. Massie ducked behind a black luxury SUV parked in front of the house next to Landon's, her knees slamming into the pavement. Pain radiated through her, and she stifled a yelp. Bean nosed her way behind a front tire.

Slowly, Massie inched her way out from behind the SUV, falling into step behind Ankle-Bird.

"Um, I know you're back there." Ankle-Bird's voice floated back to Massie. "I can smell your granny perfume."

"Ex-hu-use me?" Massie's fear tingles turned to anger. Her grip tightened protectively around Bean, who let out a delicate sneeze.

"It took Landon two bottles of puppy shampoo just to get that smell out of Bark's fur last night," Ankle-Bird said coolly.

"At least I don't smell like liver," Massie snapped, wishing she'd had more time to come up with something better.

Ankle-Bird stopped walking and whip-turned around. Instinctively, Massie took a step back, then instantly regretted it. High school girls were like dogs: They could smell fear.

Kneeling to the pavement, Ankle-Bird opened her palm,

revealing a small red liver treat. Bark lapped it up happily, and Bean squirmed in Massie's arms, desperate for her crush and a snack.

Puh-lease. No wonder Bark loved Ankle-Bird so much. Massie could have been bribing the puppy all this time too. Except she hadn't thought of that.

"Of course, torturing Bark's poor nose is nothing compared to what you did to his foot." Ankle-Bird swooped down and lifted Bark from the pavement, tucking him under her arm.

"Ehmagawd. That was an accident!" Massie could feel her cheeks starting to flush the same color as her tunic.

"Yeah?" Ankle-Bird blinked. "And what about those ugly booties? Were those an accident too?"

Those were LAYNE'S FAULT! Massie wanted to scream. Not that she had to explain herself to Ankle-Bird.

Massie's iPhone buzzed in her back pocket. Dropping Bean to the pavement, she reached for her cell. Bean scampered over to Bark and started tongue-kissing the side of his face. Puppy love was so much simpler than people love.

Claire: Hey. Think we could talk sometime this—

Massie shoved the phone back in her pocket without even finishing it. Claire would understand. She was apparently into ditching her friends for high school girls now.

"I'm just saying," Ankle-Bird continued with a self-righteous hair toss. "You did some serious damage. You're lucky those booties didn't make his fracture worse."

Guilt gripped Massie's stomach and squeezed it like Kendra's SuperJuicer5000. The fall breeze that fluttered through the trees and grass seemed to be getting colder by the second, nipping at Massie's clammy skin.

When the guilt settled, anger took its place. Who did this girl think she was? Just because she had an inked bird on her leg didn't make her a pet expert. It was like saying Dylan was qualified to be a judge on *Top Chef* just because she had the number for Happy Dragon takeout perma-scribbled on her palm.

"Excuse me, but are you Secret Service?" Massie sucked in a deep breath and planted her hands on her hips.

"What?" Ankle-Bird tilted her head slightly to the side, looking confused. "No."

"Then why are you on Obama's tail 24/7?"

Ankle-Bird chuckled, her eyes softening from icy blue to a warm sapphire.

Massie's Chanel No. 19 seared at her pressure points. Was Ankle-Bird making fun of her?

"Cute," Ankle-Bird smiled, scratching Bark's back with the tip of her boot. "Actually, I'm his physical therapist."

His what? Ankle-Bird fished two more liver treats from a pouch attached to her belt. Massie resisted the urge to snatch Bean's treat from Ankle-Bird's hand and feed it to her puppy herself. The last thing she needed was to lose Bean to Ankle-Bird too.

"My parents are Bark's vets, so when he hurt his paw I offered to do his therapy," she explained. "I'm going to NYU next fall to major in pet PT." She tucked a dark, shimmering wave behind her ear. "I'm Mary, by the way."

"Massie." Massie's lower lip dropped slightly, feeling chapped.

"I know," Mary said simply.

Suddenly, the last two weeks seemed a little clearer, like Massie's eyes had been dilated and the world around her was starting to come back into focus. But she refused to let hope inch its way to her heart. Just because Ankle-Bird was a professional didn't mean she didn't still have a major OWCH factor. Think of all the celebs who'd crushed on their employees: Britney and her agent, Jude and his nanny, Madonna and her personal trainer, Madonna and her other personal trainer . . . and now Landon and his puppy PT?

"Guess Landon got two for one," she said, digging her toe into the road. "A physical therapist and a crush." She kept her eyes on the pavement, not wanting to see the truth in Ankle-Bird's pore-free face.

"Crush?" Ankle-Bird snorted, her hammered-gold chandelier earrings clinking in amusement. "No way."

Massie's head snapped up. She searched the older girl's eyes for signs that she was lying. But all she saw was a flawless liquid-liner job.

"Landon's adorable and all, but I'm not really into younger guys." Ankle-Bird grinned. "My boyfriend's a freshman at Columbia."

"Seriously?" Massie's voice shook with relief, shame, and embarrassment. Tears burned the corners of her eyes, threatening to ruin her eye makeup and her reputation. Why hadn't she kept her sunglasses on? And why hadn't she gone with waterproof mascara, today of all days?

"Seriously. You okay?" Mary stepped toward Massie and tilted her head slightly, in a way that said, *You can tell me everything. I'm leaving for college in the fall, and I'll take your shameful secrets with me.*

Massie shook her head slowly, fighting the urge to bury her face in Mary's canary yellow shoulder and sob until her insides were parched. She pursed her lips together, as if she could lock all her crush insecurities inside and keep them there.

"C'mere." Mary slid her arm around Massie's trembling shoulder, guiding her to the curb. "What's going on?" she asked, sitting down on the side of the road and patting the cement next to her. Massie sank down next to her as Bark and Bean curled up between the girls.

Maybe it was the concern in Mary's older, wiser eyes. Or maybe it was the rough warmth of Bean's tiny tongue. But suddenly, Massie couldn't hold it in any longer. Staring down at the ground, she spilled like Perez Hilton. She told Mary everything: about how she'd gotten ditched by every real crush she'd ever had. About how she was about to lose Landon too. About how the upgrade had been her idea in the first place, and now all her friends were moving full-speed ahead with older friends or crushes, while her relationship had stalled out.

When she was done, Mary nodded in a *been-there* sort of way. "Sounds like you've had a lot of crushes, but they just weren't right for you."

"Until Landon." Massie shuddered, wiping her eyes with the back of her hand.

"Yeah. He's pretty great," Mary smiled, nudging Massie's knee with hers. "Sounds like he's a way better match."

Massie nodded miserably, feeling a fresh wave of tears spring to her eyes as she thought of his Pradas.

"Plus, sounds like you actually like Landon for Landon," Mary said. "I mean, did you really like those other guys, or did you just like the idea of having a crush?"

Massie blinked, clicking through her crush history. There was Derrington, with his seasonally inappropriate wardrobe choices and embarrassing booty shake. Then there was Dempsey, who couldn't talk about anything other than Africa, the environment, and helping other people. Plus, how many soccer games had Massie sat through, her butt frozen to the bleachers, when she'd rather have been at the mall with her friends?

Was Mary more relationship-savvy than Oprah?

"The perfect guy for you isn't the one who makes you want to pretend to be someone you're not," Mary said wisely, scratching behind Bark's ears. "The perfect guy makes you want to be exactly who you are."

Massie nodded slowly, soaking up Mary's wisdom like it was La Mer moisturizer. Maybe her exes hadn't been right for her. Maybe they'd just been there to show her what she really wanted in a crush: style, an adorable puppy, and an aversion to shorts in the winter. And she'd found all those things in Landon Crane.

"Thanks," she said hurriedly, leaping off the curb. "I gotta go find something." Tucking Bean underneath her arm like a football, she fixed her gaze on Landon's mailbox and speed-headed toward her crush.

"What?" Mary called after her.

Massie closed her eyes, feeling the crisp breeze slip past her love-flushed cheeks. "Myself!"

Claire sat on the wooden bench outside the Gourmet Au Lait, wedged between Layne and Cam. She popped the plastic top off her red to-go cup and blew on the steam wafting from her hot chocolate with jumbo marshmallows. The sugary sweetness of her drink mixed with Cam's woodsy cologne and the brisk fall air was making her feel light-headed in the best possible way. Spending the afternoon with Layne and Cam was almost fun enough to make her forget that Massie hadn't responded to any of her texts. Not even the ones marked URGENT X 10.

"Wait. Wait," Cam said over a mouthful of hazelnut whipped cream, sending tiny flecks of vanilla-colored fluff into a huddle of passing holiday shoppers in Santa hats. The 24-karat sparkle in his eyes was infectious, and Claire couldn't help smiling. "Pink feathers and glitter?"

"Yup," Layne nodded, looking more proud of herself than the time she'd eaten an entire bag of horseradish-flavored jellybeans dipped in hot sauce without even touching her Coke Zero. "Booties only a mother could love." Her eyes were bright with pride and thick turquoise liner.

"Poor Bark," Claire giggled, scooting a little closer to Cam.

"For real," Cam snorted, taking a long sip of his drink. When he reemerged, a tiny dab of whipped cream was perched on the end of his nose. Claire had the sudden urge to lean over and lip-kiss the sugary fluff away. Cara, of Ninth-Grade Doug and Cara, probably would have. But Claire just wrapped her hands around her cup to warm them, hoping her friends would think it was the hot drink that was making her cheeks flush. Being this close to her crush confirmed what she already knew: Cam was the ultimate upgrade, even if he was in her same grade.

"After this, wanna hit Godiva for free samples?" A mischievous glint surfaced in Layne's eye. "This week is cherry liqueur–dipped graham crackers."

Cam made a gagging sound. Then he leaned forward and pitched his empty hot chocolate cup into the painted black wire trash can next to Layne.

"Bet you guys I eat a whole box before free sample girl gives me the evil eye."

"Kidely bake your selections add pay," Claire droned in a perfect imitation of the salesgirl's nasal tone. She laughed, reaching under the bench for her yellow Matt & Nat bowler bag. "You're on," she said, sneaking a peek at her rhinestone-encrusted Motorola.

0 NEW MSGS.

The words on the screen made Claire's shoulders slump. "But we have to make a quick stop first," she said, patting the bag in her lap. The jingling sound inside made her think of charm bracelets, which made her think of Massie, which made her slump even lower in her seat.

"Where?" Cam stuffed his hands in the pockets of his hunter green windbreaker, looking curious.

Claire shrugged, trying to look mysterious.

Layne raised her left eyebrow. It hovered over her turquoise liner like a furry inchworm.

"I'm intrigued, Lyons." She brought her cardboard cup to her lips and tilted her head back to chug the last few sips. The plastic top popped off, sending steaming hot chocolate sloshing over her waffled gray long-underwear top.

Claire and Cam lunged off the bench to avoid getting hit.

"Owwwwww." Layne wiped her face with the hem of her shirt, then dabbed gingerly at her scorched red tongue. "Buuuuuuurn."

Laughing, Claire stumbled into Cam's windbreaker, wishing she could curl up against it and stay there forever. Or at least until Massie was speaking to her again.

Claire cringed. "C'mon. Let's go," she said, slinging her bowler bag over her shoulder. She ducked around a creaking silver ladder that was leaned against the coffee bar window, where a woman was stringing up a fresh green garland tied with red ribbon. Cam and Layne followed.

"Gimme a hint," Cam whispered in her ear, sending love shivers up and down her spine. But she held strong.

"You'll seeee," she teased.

"Great. Now I can't even taste the samples." Layne wiggled her tongue pitifully, like Bean did when she wanted an extra treat.

Claire led her friends down the brick-lined sidewalk toward

the square at the end of Main Street, weaving between kids on their bikes and shopkeepers frosting their windows with fake snow. Her bowler bag felt heavy, but not as heavy as her heart did when she thought about her empty inbox. She wished Massie would text her an insult, at least. Anything was better than nothing at all.

Finally, Claire spotted their destination: the wishing fountain in the main square at the center of Westchester's bustling downtown. Surrounded by colorful, manicured flower beds, the churning stone fountain spewed frothy aqua water tinted copper by the layer of pennies that rested at the bottom.

Sometimes when Claire was downtown and found a few extra cents in the back pocket of her cords, she'd stop by the fountain to wish for little things: that she and Cam would magically be on Gchat at the same time, that Todd would quit leaving the milk carton in the fridge with nothing in it but little-brother backwash, that she'd have a good bangs day at least once that week. Today, she had way more important things to wish for. Which was why she'd come prepared.

"We're here," she announced, scoping out the fountain area for an acceptable piece of real estate. A few families had parked strollers nearby, and a skater with a Travis Barker Mohawk was doing lazy circles around the perimeter of the flower beds. Claire staked out a spot between an elderly couple and three little kids tossing Cheerios into the fountain when their mom wasn't looking.

"What's the plan?" Layne looked back and forth between Claire and the fountain.

"We're making wishes for the rest of the school year," Claire announced. So far, nothing else she'd tried to keep the PC together, happy, and drama-free had worked. So she'd have to rely on a little magic.

"Cool," Cam said supportively. He patted down his windbreaker. "Except I don't have any—"

"Not a problem." Claire crouched on the brick square and unzipped her sagging bowler bag. Inside were three plastic baggies of pennies, one for each of them. She tossed one to Cam and one to Layne, then took the last for herself.

"Ready?" she asked solemnly, pinching her first penny between her thumb and index finger. It was slightly sticky, since the only baggies she could find at home had had gummies in them at one point. "Go." She flicked the penny into the fountain and closed her eyes as it skipped across the water.

I wish my friends would stop wanting to grow up so fast.

Plink. A light breeze swept through the square, and Claire shuddered, hoping that was some sort of sign from the universe. She didn't mind the idea of ninth graders as much anymore, especially after meeting Layne's friends. But what was so wrong with being happy in eighth too?

PUH-LUUUUUUUUUUNK!

A splash of fountain water splattered Claire's kelly green angora hoodie, and her eyes snapped open.

"I WISH MY BOOTIE CAM PATENT GOES THROUGH AND I'M A BILLIONAIRE BEFORE FOURTEEN," bellowed Layne. Her baggie was completely empty.

"Layne!" Claire giggle-accused. "There were like fifty pennies in there!"

Layne shrugged. "But I really, REALLY want that one to come true."

"Too bad," Cam said slyly, flicking one of his pennies over the top of the fountain spray like he was going for the extra point in paper football. "If you say 'em out loud, they definitely don't come true."

Claire nodded in agreement.

"Wrong!" Layne lunged for Claire's baggie, digging out a handful. "I WISH CLAIRE AND CAM WOULD THINK I'M HILAAAAAARIOUS." She flung the pennies toward the fountain, and all but one rained into the water. The last one bounced off the curved edge of the fountain and onto the tan orthopedic shoe of the old lady next to Claire.

"LAYNE!" Claire and Cam burst out laughing. "QUIT IT!" Claire apology-shrugged at the old lady, who gripped her husband's hand and shuffled to the other side of the fountain.

"See?" Layne spread her arms open wide. "You laughed."

Claire shook her head, closing her eyes again. *I wish Cam and Layne and I will never stop being friends. Ever.* In the midst of all the PC drama, Cam and Layne were her tried-and-trues, the friend equivalents of Massie's go-to Citizen boot-cuts and black BCBG cami.

Claire opened her left eye, sneaking a peek at Cam. He was winding up for another wish. She closed her eye again. *I wish Cam and I are wishing the same things.*

Plink.

"I WISH I GET THE LEAD IN THE SPRING MUSICAL AND GET DISCOVERED BY AN INDIE AGENT AND GET FAMOUS AND START MY OWN LINE OF CUSTOM-DECORATED SNEAKERS," Layne yelled.

"You don't even have any pennies left," Claire murmured out of the corner of her mouth. Then another wish popped into her mind.

I wish Massie would stop being mad at me for liking my crush so much and wanting other friends.

Plink.

A lump rose in Claire's throat. It felt like she was trying to swallow a jumbo marshmallow but couldn't. Immediately, tears stung her eyes, and she opened them, feeling the weight of her social dilemma drag her down like a million bags of pennies. Why did everything have to be so complicated? Why couldn't she just pick her own friends and her own crush, and be happy?

Layne sidled over to Claire, giving her a silent side-hug. It was like she understood without Claire having to say a word.

"Thanks," Claire sniffed, rapid-blinking her tears away before Cam saw them. But he was still dutifully flicking his pennies into the water, his eyes screwed shut. Claire felt a fresh rush of love for her crush.

"Hey. You wanna hang out with me and Cara and Syd this afternoon?" Layne asked. "There's a matinee at the Westchester Community Theater."

"Maybe. What show is it?"

"Westchester Side Story." Layne grinned. "It's the little kid production. Syd directed it, so we're all going."

Claire nodded uncertainly. Part of her just wanted to go home, curl up on her couch, and forget this week ever happened.

"And then afterward we're all hanging out. It'll be fun."

Cam opened his eyes, stuffing his penny bag in the pocket of his windbreaker. "Count me out," he volunteered. "I had to go to my cousin's kindergarten school play last week. And videotape it." He shuddered at the memory.

"So?" Layne turned to Claire. "Up for a girls' night?"

Claire hesitated, staring at the ground. If only it were as simple as Layne was making it sound. Sure, the older girls were cool, and hanging out with them at the auction had been fun. But how could she possibly have a good time with new friends, when Massie's text-silence was so loud she could barely think straight?

She closed her eyes and pinched another penny from the bag, flinging it desperately into the fountain.

I wish I didn't have to choose.

Massie's and Bean's reflections in Landon's brass door knocker made them look like giant bobblehead dolls, and Massie's insides felt just as shaky.

"Wish me luck," she murmured to her puppy, leaning closer to the polished brass for a quick gloss check. The faded sheen of her Glossip Girl Toasted Cinnamon gloss was barely visible, but re-glossing wasn't an option. In her hurry, she'd accidentally left her Spy bag with Mary and Bark. The idea of going in glossless made her feel even shakier, like she was that Brookstone massage chair and Layne had turned the dial to MAX. She lifted the heavy door knocker and held both her breath and the knocker, but she didn't let it clang down just yet.

Bean lapped at Massie's trembling cheek, centering her. Reminding her of everything Mary had told them about finding a crush who liked Massie for all the things that made her a true alpha. And of the list she'd made herself while trying to muster up the courage to knock on Landon's door.

Top Three ALPHA Things about ME:

1. Being a devoted mother to Bean and friend to the Pretty Committee, even when CERTAIN people (Kuh-laire) think they can do better.
2. Having trendsetting style (duh x 10).
3. Being a beyond-loyal crush.

So far, Landon only knew the first two things about her. What if he didn't give her a chance to prove the third? What if he decided she was too immature, and she never found another crush who—

The brass knocker slipped from her grip and slammed against the door, jolting her back to reality. She shook her head, ridding her brain of negative thoughts and tousling her hair at the same time. Landon would be beyond lucky to have an alpha like her as his crush. And if he wouldn't forgive her, she'd find the strength to move on. Landon Crane obviously wasn't the only fashion-savvy crush in the sea. If Jessica, Demi, and Posh could find their perfect matches, nothing could stop Massie from doing the exact same—

Suddenly, Massie wasn't staring at her own reflection in Landon's doorway anymore. She was staring at Landon. His turquoise eyes clouded over the second he saw her.

"Hey." She hated that her voice sounded as shaky as she felt. Her eyes traveled from Landon's dark, almost-time-to-get-a-haircut-but-not-quite waves to his Prada stretch polo and Diesel five-pocket straight-legs. He was perfection.

"Hey." But frozen the way he was in the doorway, he also looked like a hawt, angry action figure who was dressed to kill. And just might.

Massie swallowed. Couldn't he at least invite her in? Nibbling her gloss-free bottom lip, she racked her brain for acceptable next moves.

Twenty minutes ago, she would have lied through her teeth. She would have told her (ex?) crush that she had brought Bark to Pup-A-Palooza because she'd heard Landon would be there, and she'd realized that a sick puppy should never be away from his owner. Then she probably would have made something up about how the booties were approved by POOPPT (Professional Organization of Puppy Physical Therapists) and she'd special-ordered them from Finland, just for Bark. Then she would have told Landon he owed her for the booties, plus shipping and handling and delivery confirmation. Then she would have speed-walked Bean home and tweeted about how the *L* in Landon obviously stood for *LBR*.

But that was twenty minutes ago. Now, standing in the golden afternoon sunlight on Landon Crane's doorstep, Massie Block was a completely different alpha. This must have been how the Ashleys (Simpson and Tisdale) felt in their first post–nose-job paparazzi shots.

"Massie?" Landon waved his hand in front of her face. The spicy citrus notes of his CK Eternity Summer cologne piqued her senses, helping her focus.

"We need to come in." Massie shifted Bean to her other arm, scratching the exact place on Bean's forehead that made her front left paw vibrate uncontrollably. Even if Landon wouldn't say yes to Massie, he couldn't say no to Bean. "'Kay?" She instantly regretted asking permission. Alphas didn't ask. They informed.

Landon shrugged, then stepped aside. "I guess."

Stung, Massie and Bean swished past Landon into the foyer, her arm brushing against his. Despite the pain in her heart, the tiny hairs on the back of her neck stood up, screaming *true love*.

Landon's house was nothing like the Block Estate but every bit as inspired. Instead of marble floors, antique mahogany side tables, and a towering grandfather clock, Landon's entryway had scarlet walls, slate floors, and framed candids of Landon's mom Celia with some of Massie's fashion icons. Including the real Marc Jacobs.

"Marc's such a sweetheart." Celia Crane's lilting voice sounded in Massie's diamond-studded ear, making her jump. She whirled around, resisting the urge to slap her palm over her naked lips in embarrassment.

"Naming the boutique Bark Jacobs was his idea, you know." Landon's mom beamed, the wild, dark tendrils around her face accenting her high cheekbones. Celia was the picture of casual chic in a black-and-white-striped Diane von Furstenberg maxidress and chunky turquoise accessories. "Good to see you again, Massie," she said, patting the signature pawprint brooch nestled in her messy updo. "You too, Bean."

Bean yapped once, licking Celia's hand.

"Ehmagawd, hi." Massie flushed, her heart doing a jig at

the sound of Landon's mom not pronouncing her name *May-see,* like she had on the boutique's opening night. It meant Landon had been talking about her. At least before last night anyway.

Celia turned to Landon. "Just got the prototype in for the fragrance," she said, lifting a small frosted glass bottle in the shape of a pug. "Perfect, don't you think?" Without waiting for Landon to respond, Celia tilted the bottle for Massie to see. "We're doing a line of canine cologne, and Landon designed the boy puppy scent," she explained. "It'll come out with our spring line."

Massie's heart beat in double time. Designing a fragrance before he hit tenth? Impressive. She leaned in to get a closer look. The face on the bottle was the spitting image of Bark.

"What're you calling it?" she asked the bottle, wishing she could look Landon in the eye and ask him instead.

Celia glanced pointedly in Landon's direction.

"Eau Bama," Landon mumbled, picking at an invisible thread on the sleeve of his polo.

"Clever, no?" After a beat of silence, Celia glanced back and forth between Landon and Massie. Her clear blue eyes glowed with amusement.

"Okay, okay, I can take a hint," she smiled. "Business can wait. I'll be in my studio if anyone needs me." She glided barefoot across the slate floor and kissed Landon on the forehead.

"Mom." Landon rolled his eyes.

"Sorry." Celia wiped away the glossy print above Landon's

eye. "Gluten-free cookies in the oven, if you want some." And then she was gone.

Looking up, Massie saw that Landon's eyes had softened a little. But he was still silent. Waiting.

"Um, about last night." Massie's silk tunic was starting to cling to her damp skin. She dropped Bean to the floor and kept her arms tight at her sides, in case of pit stains. "I was totally planning on keeping Bark at home? But then I saw on Animal Planet that keeping puppies cooped up when they're injured actually makes them worse. Like, psychologically. They get depressed."

Landon squinted skeptically. "Huh?"

"It's called PMS," Massie lied. She was starting to sweat through her jeans, her sense of truth and purpose leaving her pores along with the salty dew. "Puppy melancholy syndrome?"

Bean nudged Massie's shin gently with her wet nose.

And Mary's voice replayed in Massie's mind.

The perfect guy makes you want to be exactly who you are.

Massie froze, feeling the same way she'd felt in the seconds before Olga had waxed her brows for the very first time. Maybe the anticipation of pain was worse than the actual pain itself.

Bean looked up and *yap*-cheered her on. Massie took a deep breath and let loose.

"ItookBarktothepartysoIcouldspyonyou'causeIdidn'ttrustyouandthoughtmaybeAnkle-Bir—I mean, Mary was your girlfriend and so Layne put these cameras in the booties and made them ugly on purpose I think, which is so like her, what an LBR, and then Bean wouldn't wear them so Bark had to, and also I just spent the last hour spying on your house from the bushes, which is psycho times ten, and the thing is, I only did all that 'cause I like you way more than any of my other crushes, who weren't right for me 'cause actually I hate soccer and Africa and charity and boys in shorts. Plus I hate bronzer too, and I don't wear heels to movie night and I actually really like trick-or-treating for the candy too, not just the costumes, and most of all I love Bean and Bark and your new fragrance which is ah-dorable by the way."

Massie stumbled back against the wall. The sound of her relieved, ragged breath filled the entry hall. She'd done it. Said everything she'd always wanted to say to her crush but couldn't.

Bean's tongue fell out of her mouth in disbelief.

Landon's eyes widened. Massie couldn't tell if it was from disbelief or panic, or whether he just thought she was insane. But hawnestly? It didn't matter. Without her insecurities weighing her down, she felt lighter than she did after a full month on the Zone. No more lies or scheming or stalking. From here on out, she was going to tell the truth. Whether Landon Crane liked it or not.

Landon blinked, still silent.

Sweeping a stunned Bean off the floor, Massie headed for the front door, waiting for Landon to call her name. Tell her he couldn't live without her. Beg her to design a girl puppy cologne, so they could start their promotional tour for Eaux Ensembles.

But all she heard was her puppy's steady pant and the thump of her own heart. Her insides seized, and for a split second, a wave of regret threatened to overcome her. She swallowed it, along with her pride and the last remaining bit of Toasted Cinammon gloss on her parched lips. Then she yanked open the door and stepped into the light of day.

As her heels clacked against the brick steps, she wrinkled her brow. More than anything, she was confused. How could Landon let a moment like that pass him by without realizing she was the one? She took a deep breath, not sure whether she wanted to laugh or cry, or both. She was sure of one thing: If she had to do it all over again, she would.

Her iPhone buzzed in her back pocket, and she pulled it out, preparing for Claire's billionth text. But the name on the screen wasn't Claire's.

Landon: I H8 bronzer 2. ☺

Before Massie could reread the text to make sure it wasn't a truth-induced hallucination, Landon's front door opened. He stood just inches away and locked eyes with her as his fingers flew over the keypad on his cell.

Her phone buzzed again. It took all her bodily strength to tear her gaze from his long enough to look down at her phone.

Landon: 4given. ☺

He may as well have sent her a text filled with nothing but hearts, because that was all she saw. Landon Crane liked her. Her. *Ehmagawd*s, gloss-free lips, and insecurities included.

They locked eyes again, and her entire body felt like she was back in the Brookstone chair. But in a good way this time. Telling Landon everything was obviously going to bring them closer. So why should she stop with him? Why not tell all her friends the truth? Massie had a feeling she was on to something.

She decided to start with Claire. Tell her that if she wanted to stay with Cam instead of upgrading, she could. Tell her that she understood why Claire hadn't wanted to upgrade in the first place. For one—

Massie looked up. Landon was moving slowly toward her, his eyes screaming, *I am so gonna lip-kiss you right now*. As if on cue, a chilly breeze swept between them, finger-combing Massie's hair. The clouds overhead parted, and golden sunlight drenched the front stoop. And Bean leapt from Massie's arms, running in tight circles around them as if to push them closer together.

It was perfect. Except for one thing.

Massie's stomach lurched into her throat, like she might vom.

As Landon leaned in, his eyelids getting heavy, warning sirens blared in Massie's brain. She wasn't prepared for this! She wasn't even glossed! And she had no idea how to lip-kiss a ninth-grader! Did they do it differently? Why hadn't she asked Mary when she'd had the chance?

"EhmagawdIhavetogotalktoClairelikerightnow," she blurted, sidestepping Landon before he could get any closer.

Landon's eyes snapped open, and he gave her a shy smile.

"'Kay?TextyoulatertellyourmomIsaidbye." Massie stumbled down the front steps, Bean at her heels.

Striding down the drive toward the street, she kept her gaze focused straight ahead, torn between wanting to turn around, wanting to run, and wanting to Google Video ninth-grade lip-kissing on her iPhone. She hoped Landon knew that the kiss dis was nothing personal. She just wasn't ready yet. And if he liked her as much as his lovesick Efron eyes said he did, he'd understand. He had to.

CURRENT STATE OF THE UNION	
IN	**OUT**
Text messages	Subliminal messages
Confessing	Obsessing
Kiss-dissing Landon	Lip-kissing Landon

"Wooooooooooo-hooooooooooooooooooooo!" Layne hooted in Claire's ear as Syd led a stumbling chain of costumed third-graders across the Westchester Community Theater stage for their fourth bow. The applause in the small theater reached a frenzied pitch, making Claire hear a buzzing sound. And she'd lost all feeling in her neck sometime between "Tonight" and "I Feel Pretty," since as VIP guests of the director, Claire, Layne, and Cara had gotten to sit in the front row, tilting their heads back at a 90-degree angle for the production.

On the other side of Layne, Cara leaned forward in her seat, her blond waves skimming her knees. "Aren't they ador-able?" she called, her cheeks flushed from the stale warmth that hovered over the creaky theater seats.

Claire nodded. To her right, a middle-aged man holding a blinking camcorder turned and smiled proudly.

"THAT'S MY GIRL!" he yelled, waving a cellophane-wrapped bouquet of roses at the herd of little girls on stage.

Congratulations, mouthed Claire politely. She let her eyes dart down to her cell, which had been resting on her left thigh ever since she'd taken her seat. No calls, no texts . . . not even a Twitter update or a Facebook posting. She yanked up the sleeves on her hoodie, needing some air.

It wasn't like calling Massie again would make her pick up. And by now, Claire was too exhausted and confused to figure out why her friend wasn't responding. Was she mad that Claire had hung with Syd and Cara last night? Too busy having fun with Landon to answer? Or just generally hurt that Claire had been looking for friends outside the Pretty Committee?

The applause started to settle, and Claire shook the ringing from her ears. Looking perfectly at home under the white-hot theater lights, Syd was holding a bouquet of flowers and a program. She waited for the shouts of proud parents to die down, then spoke into the lapel mic on her black cowl-neck sweater. Claire craned her neck again, staring up Syd's oval-shaped nostrils.

"Thanks to everyone for supporting this year's production." Syd's voice boomed throughout the theater, commanding the audience's attention. "We hope you enjoyed the show. Just a couple notes, and then we'll wrap up. Don't forget, opening night for the main-stage show *Beauty and the Beast* is coming up, so get your tickets. And auditions for the spring musical, *Little Shop of Horrors,* will be held in—"

"Daddy loves you, Michelle!" the stage dad next to Claire called out.

A giggle rippled through the audience. On stage, Michelle widened her eyes in humiliation and ran to hide behind Syd.

". . . will be held in two weeks," Syd smiled into her shoulder, swatting the little girl's head with a program. "Thanks, and have a great afternoon." The kids took another bow and a dusty-smelling velvet curtain careened from the rafters, sweeping across the stage.

If Claire had a mic of her own, she would have sprinted to the Block Estate to explain everything at top volume. How she'd never meant to hurt Massie or the Pretty Committee. How the upgrade had made her feel like she had no other choice but to find friends who accepted her, eighth-grade crush and all.

But most of all, Claire wanted Massie to know that hanging with Syd and Cara was starting to make her change her mind about having older friends. That maybe Massie had been right, after—

"So what're we doing after?" Layne said, interrupting her thoughts. Claire hadn't even noticed Layne standing over her, clogging the aisle as parents jostled to get to the steps that led up to the stage.

Cara shrugged, flicking a piece of blond hair away from her eyes. "Wanna go see a movie?"

"Meh." Layne didn't look enthused.

Claire checked her phone again.

"Girls!" Syd hurried out from behind the curtain and eased onto the stage, swinging her legs over the edge and depositing an armful of bouquets next to her. "So . . . ?" Her baby blue eyes sparkled with excitement.

"Inspired," Layne decided grandly.

"Couldn't have been cuter." Cara fanned herself with a folded program.

"Totally." Claire nodded, wishing Massie wasn't hogging all her attention from somewhere across town.

Syd bowed dramatically. When she swung upright again,

she pushed a brunette lock behind her ear and looked at Claire.

"So whadja think?" she prompted with a kind smile.

I think I've had enough drama to last me a lifetime. Claire used her palm as a visor to shield her eyes from the beaming stage lights. "About . . . ?"

"*Little Shop* auditions! You in?"

"I'm definitely thinking about it." Claire sideswiped her bangs.

"I still have to find a song," Cara announced. "I'll probably do 'Suddenly Seymour.'" She tilted her head back, closed her eyes, and broke into song in the middle of the crowded theater. In seconds, Layne and Cara joined in. Even Claire sang along, relaxing into her chair a little: "Suddenly Seymour! Is standing beside you! You don't need no makeup! Don't have to preteeeeeeend!"

"You know it!" Cara grinned. "Cool."

Claire nodded. "It's one of the songs on my show tunes karaoke mach—" She cut herself off, hoping the parents' chatter and the slapping of little-kid feet up and down the aisles had drowned her out.

But Syd and Cara didn't roll their eyes at her or shoot her down with a snappy comeback. Instead, they leaned forward in excitement, chattering at the same time.

"You have a karaoke machine!" Cara gasped. "No way! I've always wanted one of those!"

"Can we go try it out?" Syd plucked her lapel mic from her collar. "Like, now?"

"I call first song!" Layne smacked the stage with her palm.

Claire burst into relieved laughter. This was definitely not the reception she'd been expecting. She'd only mentioned singing karaoke to the PC one time since moving to Westchester, and it had been her last. The Pretty Committee had shot it down with the speed and precision of a highly trained firing squad. Massie pinky-swore up and down that the word *karaoke* was Japanese for *LBR*. Alicia said if anybody at OCD ever found out Claire even brought it up, she'd be forced to move to Spain to live with her cousins, as part of the Westchester Protection Program. Kristen said she'd rather be playing soccer, and Dylan had come down with bad sushi poisoning.

"CLAIRE!" Layne, Cara, and Syd yelled, bringing her back. "Let's go!"

Syd jumped off the stage, landing with a thud next to Claire. "I can have my stuff together in five. Meet you outside." She hurried off to the dressing rooms, belting the second verse to "Suddenly Seymour" at the top of her lungs.

"'Kay." Claire laughed, feeling the girls' enthusiasm start to wash away her bad mood.

Layne grabbed Claire's wrist and jerked her to standing. "Hurry it up, Chuck!"

"Coming!" Claire followed Layne and Cara down the theater aisle toward the exit. Maybe now she could finally leave the drama behind.

Massie Block was a changed alpha. And not just on the inside. Her creamy-white cashmere Raw 7 sweater dress, delicate platinum accessories, and crackled metallic flats announced to the Block Estate and surrounding areas that she was cleansed. Purified of all her insecurities, fears, and doubts. Except the ones about lip-kissing ninth-grade boys. But she'd deal with those later. For now, she had more important Pretty Committee business to attend to. First stop: the guesthouse.

She pumped the shiny handle on the sunroom door once, and a fresh flood of chilly afternoon air surrounded her. The late afternoon light seemed almost transparent, highlighting her bronze-free cheekbones, iced pout, and shimmer-accented browbone like she was a rare jewel on display at the Smithsonian.

Stepping outside, Massie closed the sunroom door behind her and glided over the freshly trimmed lawn, not worrying the slightest bit about grass stains ruining her all-white ensemble.

Even her white D&G quilted leather Miss Glamorous bag felt lighter than usual. Inside, she'd packed only the necessities: her subliminal confidence CD (kindling for the friendship bonfire she'd scheduled later that night, to renew her bonds with the PC and start fresh with her crush), a new tube of Glossip Girl First Snow gloss, and a small bag of gummies as a peace offering for Claire.

I wanted you to upgrade 'cause I thought if you didn't, it meant we weren't friends anymore. But now I get why you don't want to. For one thing, Cam's pretty cute. More in a cheek-pinching kind of way than a lip-kissing kind of way, but still. Plus, high school boys can be kind of scary. Trust me, I get that now.

Massie paused mid-apology, practicing giving Claire time to respond. Then she continued.

Ehmagawd, forgiven! I missed you too! No more fighting or lies. Pinky-swear.

The lights were on in the living room, making the guest-house glow. Inside, Claire was probably practicing her own apology in the mirror over the wing chair in the corner. Massie's steps quickened, bringing her closer and closer to a reconciliation with her friend.

The grass seemed to be shaking with anticipation the closer Massie got to the guesthouse. Confused, she paused in her tracks. Tiny vibrations were shooting from the ground and through her flats, traveling to her heart. The delicate platinum hoops in her ears trembled, like a minor earthquake had struck the backyard of the Block Estate. And the faint sounds of deaf cats dying a slow, tortured death leaked from the guesthouse walls.

"Ehmagawd, Kuh-laire!" Massie plugged her ears and

squinted toward the living room window. Then she picked up her pace, her heart fearing the worst. Nothing good could possibly be happening anywhere near that agonizing—

Finally getting a closer glimpse into the living room windows, Massie froze like she was a perfectly styled ice sculpture someone had accidentally left outside. She'd feared the worst, but nothing could have prepared her for what was happening inside. She darted the final few feet to the window and crouched in the bushes, temporarily forgetting her no-more-stalking rule.

If she hadn't just finished a fresh mascara application—waterproof this time—she would have rubbed her eyes, to make sure she wasn't seeing things.

On the other side of the chilled glass panes, Claire, Layne, and the ninth-grade girls from last night's party were in the middle of the living room, each gripping a "microphone" with one hand and flailing wildly with the other. All the furniture had been moved to the edges of the room, and the karaoke machine by the fireplace flickered with lyrics to a song Massie couldn't make out.

It had to be a show tune, though, because normal music didn't call for this kind of epileptic fit. Leave it to Claire to be a ninth-grade LBR magnet. Massie leaned closer, pressing her palms against the chilled glass. Giggling and dancing to the music, Claire's cheeks were flushed. And not in a cheek stain–induced way, but in a real way. Damp bangs matted to her forehead, she looked . . . happy. Like Massie and the Pretty Committee were the last things on her mind.

Massie's insides hardened. So Claire hadn't been apologizing to her mirror. Instead, she'd been cheating on her with Layne and two ninth-grade theater geeks.

Throat tightening, Massie's palms slid down the dewy panes, leaving wet streaks that looked like tears. The heaviness she'd felt just hours ago came barreling back, seeming to bolt her to the ground outside the guesthouse. How could Claire have recast her this quickly? It was as if Massie had died, and Claire hadn't even waited until after the funeral to find new friends.

Hot tears formed at the corners of Massie's amber eyes. So this was what she meant to Claire. Nuh-thing. She'd been easier to replace than an old blush brush. And not the Shu Uemura kind, with the softer-than-soft mink bristles. The synthetic kind, from Duane Reade. The kind Claire would buy.

Finally, she couldn't hold the tears back anymore, and they slid down her cheeks like tiny rivers of betrayal. Watching Claire and her upgrades laughing and dancing together was torture, like getting a full-body wax in slow motion. But somehow, Massie couldn't bring herself to look away.

Crouched behind the worn, mustard-colored couch in the living room, Claire gripped her cordless flat iron and giggle-bounced in perfect sync with her backup singers, waiting for her cue.

"Uh-FIVE, SIX, SEVEN, EIGHT!" Layne screeched into the mic she'd rigged to the guesthouse surround-sound system. She was standing in the middle of the living room, directly in front of the shadeless brass floor lamp by the window that served as her spotlight.

Propped up on a blue side table in the corner, Claire's old portable karaoke machine came to life, blasting the opening beats of the intro to *Little Shop of Horrors* from the living room to the bedrooms upstairs.

Syd nudged Claire with a curling iron, and the three girls shot up, each holding their hair appliances–slash-mics to their lips.

"Little Shop! Little Shop of Horrors!" Claire bellowed into her flat iron. "Little Shop! Little Shop of Terrors!"

Shimmying around the couch, Claire, Syd, and Cara joined Layne at the karaoke mic, singing at the top of their lungs to their reflections in the living room window. Claire closed her eyes and threw her hands over her head, feeling the kind of freedom that comes with not worrying about pit stains, being on key, or what anybody else is thinking. She hadn't felt this free since . . . well, since moving to Westchester.

Claire looped her arms around the ninth-grade girls, pulling them in for the final verse. She didn't even bother fiddling with her bangs, which were sweat-laminated to her forehead. With every note, she released some of the tension that had been building up inside of her ever since Massie had first mentioned the upgrade. Slowly, her shoulders were starting to inch from her CZ-adorned ears back to their normal position.

"Little Shop! Little Shop of Horrors! No, no, no, no, no, noooooooooooo!" Claire belted.

"CLLLLLLLAAAAAAAAAAAAAAAIIIIIIIIIIIRRRRRRRRRE!" From upstairs, Todd's whine rose over the sound of the music. "TURN THAT OFF OR I'M TELLLLLLIIINNNG!"

Claire side-glanced at the other girls, and they all dissolved in laughter. Layne gyrated over to the karaoke machine, cranking up the volume even louder.

"WE CAN'T HEEAAAR YOOOUUU!" she screamed, wiggling her hips.

As Cara threw her head back and harmonized into a travel hair dryer, her loose blond waves swinging around her shoulders, Claire caught Layne's eye.

Layne winked, saying, *Do you love 'em, or do you love 'em?*

Claire nodded. Spending time with ninth-grade girls was pretty much the same as hanging with girls in eighth, only with more cleavage and public lip-kissing. And that was kind of . . . okay.

As the song wound down, Layne programmed an ensemble

number from *Shrek: The Musical* into the machine. Whipping a cashmere throw from the wing chair in the corner, she threw it around her shoulders and free-danced around the living room like she was possessed.

Claire's stomach ached from laughing so hard. It was a signal to her brain that she'd finally found her niche. Friends who were her perfect match, even if they were older. Ashton and Demi had had it right all along: Age really was nothing but a num—

"AHHHHHHHHHHHH!" Claire screamed, suddenly catching a glimpse of a figure dressed in all white, hovering outside the frosty living room window. Her heart leapt into her throat, and she staggered backwards, slamming into an oak console table.

Massie.

"AHHHHHHHHHHHHH!" echo-sang Layne, Syd, and Cara, thinking Claire was ad-libbing. They threw their arms open wide and planted their bare feet hip's width apart.

Squinting from underneath her dampened bangs, Claire watched her friend. Massie seemed to be staring right through her, like she was made of clear lip gloss. A sharp gust of wind swished through the trees in the yard, making Massie's cream sweater dress float around her knees. Suddenly, a single, shining tear tumbled down Massie's cheek. And then another. And another.

Claire's throat tightened as she watched Massie crying, softly at first, then harder. Soon, her thin shoulders had started to shake. Seeing Massie Block cry reminded Claire of the time she'd seen her dad cry at Grampa Lyons's funeral. Before that moment, Claire hadn't actually believed that her dad really ever cried, except that one time during the Super Bowl. Which wasn't really the same, since those were tears of joy.

"Has anybody seen my shoes?" she yelled over the music, dropping to her knees on the carpet. But the girls didn't hear her. Claire swallowed the guilt boulder lodged in her throat. She'd only meant to branch out a little with new friends, not hurt the old ones. She was allowed to do that, wasn't she? And it wasn't like she could have invited Massie anyway, since she hadn't responded to any of Claire's texts.

Finally, she found her shoes wedged underneath the couch. She shoved her feet into them, the tongues bunched around her toes, and ran to the window.

Massie was still standing where Claire had left her. Only up close, she didn't actually look sad. Her face was turning a deeper and deeper shade of scarlet, and her hands were clenched at her sides. Her tear-filled amber eyes seared straight into Claire's.

Claire took a step back, almost tripping over her laces. Massie wasn't devastated. She was fuming.

On the other side of the glass, Massie's iridescent-glossed lips were moving slowly. Sending Claire a message. Claire leaned toward the window, glad there was a pane of glass between them and wondering if it was heel-proof. She stage-shrugged at Massie, to show she didn't understand.

In one smooth movement, Massie reached into her bag and

produced her iPhone. Without taking her burning gaze from Claire for a second, her fingers flew over the keys. Claire's Motorola buzzed in her pocket.

Massie: This. Is. War.

Claire balked at the screen, feeling like someone had just taken a blowtorch to her insides. A declaration of war? For trying to find friends that made her happy?

Tearing her eyes from Massie's, Claire whipped around and reached for her flat iron. Her heart was thumping almost as loud as the beat of the music. But it wasn't from fear, like it usually was with Massie. It was from anger.

Suddenly, the spotlight in the living room seemed brighter, the music louder. Layne's choreographed flailing seemed ten times more carefree, and Syd and Cara's smiles seemed even more genuine.

No way was Claire going to let Massie tell her who she could and couldn't be friends with. No way was she going to suffer just to make Massie feel more in charge. More alpha. Not anymore.

The girls giggle-waved Claire over to the mic. "It's the FINALE!"

Quickly, Claire composed a text of her own.

Claire: Bring. It. On.

Without even looking out the window, Claire powered off

her cell and joined the group. Wedging between her two new friends, Claire felt safe. Protected. And ready to pull the curtain on Massie Block's reign of terror.

She took a deep breath and prepared to belt out the last note of the song. But for Claire, this didn't feel like a finale. It felt like her grand debut.

What happens when THE CLIQUE's Skye Hamilton,
the original eighth-grade alpha,
gets an invite to ultra-exclusive Alpha Academy?

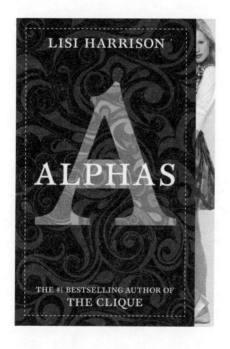

Turn the page to find out why everyone's tawking about
Lisi Harrison's newest #1 bestselling series!

Skye skipped down the plane's stairwell, downgrading her smile from high beam to low so as not to blind anyone with her excitement. Her mint, jersey-knit dance skirt ballooned up, and she shoved her hands in her skirt pockets to push it down around her long, tan legs. Just as her ballet flats made contact with the gold carpet that cut across the Jetway, the door of the private plane closed behind her.

A glass tower rose in the distance, and green caterpillar-shaped trees waved in the breeze. She arranged her white-blond wavelets behind her and blinked. Where was the welcome committee? Where was her adoring public? Where was *anyone*? She wasn't used to being alone. It was her unwritten policy to have people around her at all times. The silence made her felt a little lost and a little grown-up all at once, like the first time she'd flown by herself to visit her grandma in Florida.

Fishing her aPod out of her purse, she kept her eyes glued on the horizon, searching for signs of life.

"Follow the gold carpet," a honeyed Australian voice piped in.

There, on the rectangular screen of her aPod, was Shira's face framed by her famous red waves. Heel-toeing along the carpet, which sparkled like a thousand Swarovski crystals, Skye felt like Dorothy in Oz—only she never wanted to go home.

The carpet led her through a thicket of Joshua trees, and when she emerged on the other side of the green pine curtain, she found herself staring at a pink sand beach and what appeared to be miles of blue water.

"Ohmuhgud," she gasped, noticing the high-def rainbow up ahead.

WHOOOOOOO!

A translucent train that looked like a massive string of see-through pearls slithered along the sand and stopped in front of her. Skye tried to scope out the other girls, but all she saw was the back of their blowouts as they climbed inside their personal train cars.

Was a student body more alpha than OCD's even possible? And if it was, what did it look like? September *Vogue*? She was gagging to know. Or was the bitter taste of chocolate in the back of her throat the jet's mini cupcakes going AWOL after the private plane ride?

Once inside, Skye settled into an egg-shaped Lucite

chair. An identical one faced her; only it was empty. For a moment Skye tried to imagine who she would want joining her on this dreamlike adventure, if she could pick one person to fill the seat. She ran through her long list of friends, boyfriends, and dance friends. But no one from the past seemed good enough for the future. Not even her perfect mother. Not when the future looked like *this*! Why wear last year's dance shoes in next year's recital?

A small silver wheel next to the chair turned like a mini Ferris wheel, rotating an assortment of mini snacks—tiny bags of veggie chips, bite-size brownies, and those mini candy bars that kids get at Halloween—the kind Skye had never outgrown and loved year round. Miniatures made her feel like she was larger than life, like the world was in the palm of her hand.

She grabbed a tray of mini beakers filled with colored water—blue, purple, pink, and yellow—and took a sip. They looked like drinkable glow sticks and tasted like candy. Then she turned her attention to the @-shaped map that suddenly appeared before her.

A blinking gold arrow next to the words *Skye Hamilton is here* was flash-traveling from the opening of the circle toward the *a* inside. Skye fought the urge to press her glossed lips to the train's window to get a better view of the mirage-like oasis that rose out of the dusty desert. Clear water and palm trees were whisking by. She was moving!

"Welcome to Alpha Academy, Skye." Shira Brazille,

dressed in a single-shouldered black Grecian dress and dark round sunglasses, suddenly appeared in the other chair.

Skye gasped, and then giggled nervously.

"Oh, hi, Ms. Brazille." She choked back the bitter taste of chocolate once again. "It's a total honor to meet you!" Right hand out like a true professional, Skye leaned forward to shake Shira's hand, but her fingertips went straight through the Australian mogul and she fell to the floor.

"You cannot interface with this hologram," a stern British accent warned.

Skye straightened back up, concealing her blushing cheeks behind a wall of blond hair.

Shira cackled. "Nothing is ever what it seems, is it?" She kept laughing, like this was some practical joke they'd been pulling on each other for years.

Skye faced the window, urging her cheeks to transition from fuchsia back to rosy glow.

"My campus is inspired by the Acropolis," Shira's hologram explained as they zipped past palm leaves that turned to cherry blossoms like someone had hit "replace all." Seconds later the heavy pink blooms turned to flowering cacti.

"What is this place?" Skye marveled. She had been to the actual Acropolis and seen the ruins with her parents, but there was nothing Greek looking about the super-futuristic architecture springing up around her like pages in a pop-up book. Instead of marble structures crumbling, glass towers soared. The scenery reminded her of dancing—fluid and ever-evolving.

"Behold the Pavilion," Shira bellowed as they passed an oblong structure with white steel wings stretching out from its center, like a phoenix rising.

"It has bris soleil—sunshades that open and close depending on the amount of sunlight."

As if on cue, the building's wings began to flap, creating breezy shade.

"Ohmuhgud." Skye blinked her eyelids sharply, trying to snap a mental picture for her friends and family back home. No matter how many international dance tours her mother had been on, she had definitely never seen anything like this.

"The Pavilion is the central gathering place. Inside are the health food court, shops, lounges, the spa, and a salon. You won't need money to buy anything. Just good grades, which have a monetary value and will be immediately deposited in your personal account—you access it through your aPod. You can eat for a week off an A. But an F will leave you skinnier than salmonella. It's just like life, m'dear. You fail, you starve."

Skye giggled on the off chance that Shira was joking.

"You'll notice that all the structures here are curved." Hologram Shira pointed out the Zen Center (a giant building shaped like a cross-legged Buddha), the harp-shaped Music Hall, and the ark-shaped zoo full of endangered animals. "There are no angles at Alphas—in the architecture, anyway." Shira threw her head back and laughed. She didn't have a single filling in her entire mouth.

The train looped into the ultramodern Tokyo Times Square-esque area, located to the north of the Pavilion. WELCOME SKYE! scrolled across each electronic billboard. Then the digital letters morphed into different images of her dancing. Skye's performance at Juilliard last summer, showcases at Body Alive, home movies of her and her mother performing a pas de deux. A cell phone video of her and the DSL Daters freestyling. Were the girls in the other bubbles seeing this, or did they have their own greatest-hits reels?

Shira's hologram gestured out the window to a vertical farm, with each floor housing a different crop, from super fruits like açaí berries to staples like green beans or those adorable little grape tomatoes. "Alphas is one hundred percent green. Solar panels power the island, and every building is smart and energy efficient."

"Just like you," Skye joked. But the hologram didn't get it. Instead, it stared straight at her with a *let me know when you're done doing amateur stand-up so I can continue* glare. "Sorry." Skye bit her bottom lip.

As the bubble train rounded another corner, rows of empty snow globe–shaped domes emerged. The train pulled closer, and Skye realized that there were no defining house numbers or street names to identify the residences, just the glittery autographs of the alpha females the houses were named for radiating off the glass.

Skye clapped her hands together. Where else would Oprah, Hillary Clinton, Beyoncé, Mother Theresa, and Virginia Woolf be neighbors?

"Welcome to your new home." Shira's image began to fade. "It may look yabbo on the outside, but trust me—it's quite different once you get in."

The doors opened with *boop*, releasing Skye and a carload of chilled air in front of a house marked JACKIE O. Waves of heat threatened to melt her like Pinkberry, but the glass door of her new home sensed her presence and slid open.

Inside, the house was divided into three floors, connected by a sweeping glass staircase that ran along the side of the circular walls. Skye raced through, squealing for joy with each new discovery. The collection of the original Jackie O's glasses encased in glass, the smart kitchen with a giant touch screen full of snack options, the home theater complete with stage and lighting board, the Vichy shower bathroom, the study lounge with massage chairs, the walk-in uniform closet filled with an array of metallic-colored separates, the lap pool!

"Hello?" Skye called, hoping to share the excitement with a real person.

Next, she headed up a seemingly floating glass staircase anchored by transparent glass to the bedroom upstairs. The space was wide open and loftlike, with a giant dome skylight that filled the room with light. Five canopied beds were arranged in a horseshoe, each dressed up in a fluffy white comforter.

"Phew," she muttered, relieved. Five beds meant five girls. She wouldn't be alone forever.

"Life is either a daring adventure or nothing," said an uplifting female voice.

"Hullo?" Heart thumping, Skye scanned the room. "Who said that?"

"Helen Keller," said the voice. "I was quoting her." An extremely tall woman in a pale yellow tunic appeared before her. Her face was surprisingly delicate, with small features framed by long, wavy blond locks. She looked like she was carved from butter.

"Um, hi?" Skye stuck her hand out in greeting, not because she was formal like that, but because she needed to know if it would go right through the woman.

It didn't.

Butter shook so firmly, Skye's fingers felt like they were being stuffed into a pointy-toe boot.

"I'm Thalia, the house muse. I will provide inspiration guidance to you and"—Thalia homed in on something behind Skye—"Allie J, our alpha poet laureate! Welcome."

Allie J, the reclusive yet beyond-successful songwriter!? Skye whiplashed around. *It was!*

She'd always assumed Allie J's reclusiveness was due to some kind of unseemly skin condition, like hairy-mole disease. But it wasn't. Her mole had total Crawford appeal, and her hair was black, shiny, and on her head. Even her bare feet seemed somewhat maintained and remarkably clean. How could someone pay so much attention to her in-person image and absolutely none to her Web presence? After all, beauty fades, but JPEGs are forever.

Skye reached for her ankle and pulled it toward her butt. A fiery sensation coursed through her quad, relaxing her instantly.

"So you're one of *those*." Allie J focused her emerald eyes on Skye. Skye released her ankle curiously. How did Allie J know Skye was a nervous stretcher?

"One of *what*?"

"A *dancer*. You can just tell. Dancers have the best posture." Allie J bent over and rubbed Purell between her toes.

"Oh." Skye giggled. "Yeah, thanks."

"Her mother is Natasha Flailenkoff," offered the muse, while sprinkling eucalyptus on the floor by their beds.

"And you're a writer?" Skye feigned ignorance. She had, of course, heard of Allie J's little book of poetry, *Greenhouse with Envy*, her chart-climbing songwriting, and her incessant eco-blogging. But she wasn't about to gush over someone who was one J away from being a single-namer.

Allie J lifted her head. Her cheeks were bright red. "Did you actually read it?" she asked, as though she had no clue *everyone* had read it.

"We kind of had to in English class. We were studying American poets and—"

"Cool, yeah, well, don't worry if you didn't finish it," Allie J interrupted. "I'm so over talking about it anyway. Just wait for the movie musical. It's pretty much the same thing, only with music."

"Don't give up," Thalia cooed, sprinkling one last handful of eucalyptus on the floor. The bedroom smelled like a Junior Mint. "To climb steep hills requires a slow pace at first. William Shakespeare."

Skye and Allie J exchanged a side-glance and giggled.

"How about some refreshments while we wait for the others?" the muse offered, heading to the stairs before they could answer.

"What's the story with the fortune cookie?" Skye whispered, claiming the bed in the center of the semicircle.

Allie J giggle-sat beside her. "Basketball player. Injured. Turned psychology major. She couldn't live her own dream, so now she's dedicated to helping other people find theirs. She's like a Lifetime movie."

"How do you know that?"

"I scanned her." Allie J wiggled her aPod. She pressed a button labeled ALPHA ID and a series of stats scrolled over the LCD display. "Point and click at anyone on campus and it gives you their profile."

"Really?" Skye fished around the inside of her bag for her new digital best friend.

"Really." Thalia called from downstairs. "You can try it out on Andrea. I hear her coming up the walk right now."

"Oh, and she has exceptional hearing," Allie J added. "It's been documented in science journals."

Before Skye could figure out how to activate her new DBF, the girl appeared at the top of the stairs, bearing a certain resemblance to an ex-supermodel–turned–talk show host, only her eyes were light brown and her monster lashes were real. "Girls, meet Andr—"

"Call me Triple Threat," the Tyra look-alike corrected.

Skye blinked, waiting for a punch line that didn't come.

"*What?*" The girl twist-wrapped her long dark hair into a ball and stabbed a gold stick through the center. Her bone structure was so sharp she could probably shave legs with her jaw. "That's what they called me at my old school and it stuck."

"What are your threats?" A petite girl with anime-big violet eyes and beehived pink hair appeared behind her, diving into the conversation with a flawless no-splash entry. She looked like Wanda from *The Fairly OddParents*.

"I'm a mo-dan-tress."

"What's that?" Allie J asked, apparently unfamiliar with the pretend-to-know-what-someone-is-talking-about-and-Google-it-later approach.

"Model-dancer-actress," explained Triple Threat, tossing her plaid straw fedora on the empty bed on the end.

Skye was about to warn her that a hat on the bed was bad luck, but *ohmuhgud*, did she really need to be *living* with another dancer? Maybe if the hat stayed, Triple would snap a limb and end up a double threat instead.

The new arrival flopped down on the bed next to Skye and covered her eyes with the back of her hand. One second later she shot up and sighed. "I've been through so much lately—leukemia, rehab, bulimia, a fire where I saved three babies and five kittens but ended up in the ER on a breathing machine . . ." She sighed again at the memories. "But I wouldn't take back a second of it. Because it got me here. With all of you." She turned to the window slowly and started off into the distance.

Instantly, Skye felt jealous. How cool would it be to have a dark and twisted past? The press loved that sort of

thing. After all, her mother had done most of her interviews *after* the accident. Without it, she'd have been just
another super-talented dancer whom no one had ever heard
of. Meanwhile, the worst thing that had ever happened to
Skye was diving into a pool of Jell-O—a story that would
make front page of the yearbook if she was lucky.

Allie J thumb-pressed the Alpha ID button and pointed
it at the girl. Skye quickly did the same, reading the screen
in front of her.

STAGE NAME: RENEE FORADAY. REAL NAME: RACHAEL
MARTIN-MELON. GREW UP PLAYING RAYNE STORM ON THE
LONG-RUNNING ABC SOAP PERFECT STORM SINCE SHE
WAS BORN. AFTER BEING RECRUITED TO ATTEND ALPHA
ACADEMY, SHE QUIT THE SHOW AND DYED HER HAIR PINK
AS A DISPLAY OF INDEPENDENCE. HER CHARACTER IS BEING
KILLED ON A DEADLY ROLLER-COASTER RIDE DURING SWEEPS
WEEK; THE SCENES WILL BE SHOT WITH A BODY DOUBLE. SHE
HAS LOGGED MORE ACTING DAYS THAN ANY OTHER PERSON
IN THE BUSINESS AND HAS TWELVE DAYTIME EMMYS THAT
SHE KEEPS IN HER PARENTS' FREEZER IN CASE OF FIRE.

"Wait!" Allie J effused. "You're Rayne Storm? I couldn't
tell 'cause of the eyes and the hair, you know, since you're
usually super-bronzed and brunette on the show. But I love
that soap! I've never missed a single ep—"

"Really?" Skye's eyebrows shot up. "You like soaps? I thought you were all anti-TV."

"I am." The songwriter stiffened and flushed. "But, um, the producer wanted me to rewrite the opening song, so he sent me a few seasons on DVD so I could get a feel for the show."

"So you know Bethany Condon?" Renee slapped her heavily ringed hand against her heart. "She's been like a stepmother to me."

"Yeah." Allie J blushed again. "Did I say *he* sent me tapes?"

"Yip." Triple raised an over-plucked eyebrow.

"I meant *she*," Allie J insisted. "I sometimes drop my S's—you know, to conserve energy."

Skye glanced at the empty bed. Who next? The girl responsible for the Internet? A fourteen-year-old Navy SEAL? Hermione? These girls were *better* than September *Vogue*, and Skye felt like an April Fool for having thought she'd out-fabulous them just by showing up. Skye mentally wrote her next Hope And Dream.

HAD No. 2: Survive.

Read the rest of the #1 bestselling ALPHAS, available now.

And to hear Allie J sing "Global Heartwarming," visit alphasacademy.com

When you're the daughter of
a celebrity, it's important to know
who your true friends are.

Meet Lizzie, Carina, and Hudson. . . .

They didn't ask for fame.
They were born with it.

the
daughters

by JOANNA PHILBIN

COMING MAY 2010

poppy

Available wherever books are sold.   www.pickapoppy.com   BOB218A

Welcome to Poppy.

A poppy is a beautiful blooming red flower
(like the one on the spine of this book). It is also
the name of the home of your favorite books.

Poppy takes the real world and makes it
a little funnier, a little more fabulous.

Poppy novels are wild, witty, and inspiring.
They were written just for you.

So sit back, get comfy, and pick a Poppy.

poppy

www.pickapoppy.com

THE A-LIST
HOLLYWOOD ROYALTY

gossip girl

THE CLIQUE

ALPHAS

SECRETS OF MY
HOLLYWOOD LIFE

the it
girl

POSEUR

U Ɔ

THESE
BOOTS
ARE
MADE
FOR
STALKING

poppy
pickapoppy.com

THE CLIQUE

THE CLIQUE

1. Choose a tattoo design. Carefully cut around the design with scissors.
2. Remove the clear, protective sheet from the top of the tattoo.
3. Press the tattoo facedown onto clean, dry skin. It should stick a little bit.
4. Using a wet paper towel or washcloth, thoroughly wet the back of the tattoo.
5. Wait 30 seconds for the tattoo to set.
6. Carefully peel off the paper backing and pat the tattoo dry.

To remove your tattoo, apply rubbing alcohol or baby oil to loosen the adhesive. Use a soapy washcloth to scrub off the tattoo.

WARNING: Do not apply tattoos to sensitive skin or near the eye area. Stop use if skin redness or rash develops.

Ingredients: Acrylate/VA Copolymer, Castor Oil, Ethyl Cellulose, Refined Shellac, Hydroxypropyl Cellulose, Titanium Dioxide, Carbon Black Pigment, FD&C Yellow #5 Aluminum Lake, FD&C Blue #1 Aluminum Lake, FD&C Red #7 (Calcium) Lake.

Safe and nontoxic.

Tattoos manufactured in the U.S.A.

Art © blue67/Shutterstock
Art © Didou/Shutterstock
Art © Karina Cornelius/Shutterstock
Art © SPYDER/Shutterstock
Art © Viacheslav A. Bryksin/Shutterstock
Art © xlt974 /Shutterstock

poppy
pickapoppy.com